Murder With a Side of Bacon

An Ivy Clark Mystery

Kristy Dixon

Murder With a Side of Bacon (An Ivy Clark Mystery, book-1)

Copyright © 2024 by Kristy T Dixon

All rights reserved.

No part of this publication may be reproduced, distributed, or transmitted in any form or by any means, including photocopying, recording, or other electronic or mechanical methods, without the prior written permission of the publisher, except as permitted by U.S. copyright law. For permission requests, contact kristydixon35@gmail.com.

The story, all names, characters, and incidents portrayed in this production are fictitious. No identification with actual persons (living or deceased), places, buildings, and products is intended or should be inferred.

Book Cover by Mariah Sinclair

Edited by Jenny Sims

1st edition 2024

ISBN 978-1-960841-21-6 Paperback

For Heidi Penrod and Elizabeth Thompson

Chapter 1

I didn't want to move to a small town in Kansas to help my aunt Linda with her diner, but I couldn't leave her short-staffed after her car crash. Her brakes had given out, and her old Chevy had bolted down a hill and crashed into a tree, crushing her leg. Of all my relatives, Linda was the last one I wanted to spend time with, but family was family, so I needed to be there for her.

Muddy Creek, Kansas, only has eight hundred people, which was at least twenty thousand less than I would like. I enjoyed visiting for a week or two, but anything more made me antsy. From what my mom said, Linda would need me for at least two months.

I was only a little less excited to see my cousin Tania. She was Aunt Linda's only child, and a little spoiled for my taste. We had fun together as kids, but had little in common as we got older. Tania only liked people who benefited her, so she didn't have time for me. She moved to New York City to start a modeling career but returned to Muddy Creek a year later when she hadn't immediately broken into the industry.

I pulled my red Honda Fit up to Linda's Diner and took a deep breath. Linda didn't waste time. She wanted me to go straight here instead of to her house. Tania was going to meet me. I got out of the car and stretched my back. It had been a long drive from Arizona, and I wished I could take a nap. I didn't drive straight here, but I was still exhausted.

The diner looked exactly the same as it had two years ago. A large sign with big cursive letters hung above the front doors. When I was younger, it was called Grammy Sue's Diner, but after my grandmother passed away and Linda inherited it, it became Linda's Diner. The brick building was old but well-kept. I pushed open one of the large glass doors and squinted when I went inside.

I looked around the diner, noticing the new red upholstery on the booth benches. The same jukebox that had been here since Gramma Sue ran the place sat in one corner. It had never worked but was a fun addition to the retro theme. Framed records decorated the walls, and a chalkboard displayed the menu for the day. A counter sat against one wall with stools pushed up against it.

"Ivy!" my cousin Tania exclaimed, pushing a short piece of brown hair behind her ear. She came out from behind the counter, pulling a white apron off and tossing it on a barstool. "It's about time. I almost thought you weren't coming."

"It takes a while to drive."

"I'm sure," she said, rolling her eyes.

I glanced around the diner once more. Only two tables were being used.

"The clean aprons are in the back," Tania told me. "Do you remember things from the last time you came?"

I'd only helped for a few days, and all I had done was wash tables. "I think so."

"Great. I'm gonna take off. You're in charge."

Tania's long, fake eyelashes distracted me for a minute. Tania always looked perfect. I secretly wanted fake lashes, but wasn't up for the maintenance. I blinked. "Wait, what? I thought I was helping you?"

She tilted her head and looked at me like I was dense. "You are helping me. You're helping by taking over the diner while I take care of my mom."

"All I've ever done is clean the tables."

"You're just here to make sure everything runs smoothly. It's not rocket science. Just be the boss. Being the boss is all about delegation."

Panic flooded my body. I wasn't an introvert, but I wasn't an extrovert either. I wasn't the type to come into a place and start bossing around people I didn't know. They all had to know their jobs a lot better than I did. I didn't know their jobs at all!

Tania ran her fingers through her chin-length hair and rolled her eyes again. "You look like a scared puppy. It's not that hard. You have my cell if you need anything. Just go put on an apron and get to it."

I swallowed and watched a teenage server pour water into a customer's glass. "Why do I need an apron if I'm not cooking or serving?"

"We only have one cook on this shift and one server. It's slow right now, but occasionally something happens, and they need help. You'll be fine. You make all the calls."

"Hey, José!" Tania called, causing me to jump. Behind the counter was a long rectangular window, and the cook was busy stirring something back there. He glanced out at Tania. "You remember my cousin Ivy? She's in command. Got that, José?" He nodded. "I'm off." Tania waved and was out the door in a flash.

I stood in the diner feeling ridiculous. My green T-shirt and jeans didn't mark me as the boss. I probably looked like a mess. José glanced out at me, then away. I remembered him from the last time I was here. He was around fifty, with short black hair covered in a hairnet. The server was new. She couldn't be over eighteen. She had a red ponytail and a friendly smile. Her name tag said Livy.

I walked over to the right and followed the bathroom sign. I wasn't sure if I should tell José and Livy what I was doing, but I doubted they cared. Yellow walls greeted me, and I glanced at myself in the mirror. Cold water poured out of the faucet, and I splashed some on my cheeks, avoiding my eyes so I wouldn't smear my makeup. I pulled a hairband from my wrist and pulled my long blond hair into a quick braid. I didn't even look in the mirror to see the results. Without a brush, it would not be pretty.

I left the bathroom and felt slightly bitter. I knew Linda needed help, but she could have at least let me have today to rest and get settled in. Tania should have stayed and given me more direction. Being here with no knowledge of the business seemed pointless.

Nothing was happening in the dining area, so I headed around the counter and entered the kitchen. José looked up from his stew. "Good to see you again, Miss Ivy. Do you remember me?"

I smiled. "Yes, it's nice to see you again. Is there anything I can help with?"

José shrugged. "You know how Linda is with the menu. There isn't much to it."

I nodded. Linda didn't believe in complicating things. There wasn't an actual menu at Linda's Diner. There was one option a day for breakfast, one for lunch, and one for dinner. The only choices a person could make were whether they wanted skim milk, 2 percent, Coke, or Sprite. Dessert was carrot cake every day. I asked my mom how Linda stayed in business, and she said you didn't have to try when you were the only place to eat in town. Linda was lucky José was such a superb cook.

When Gramma Sue had run the diner, there were delicious milkshakes. Some of my favorite memories of this place were of me sitting at the counter with an enormous chocolate fudge shake. Linda didn't want to deal with ice cream. She thought it was too messy.

"Let me make a dessert," I offered. "I'm not the best at cooking things like dinner, but I love to bake. I have a chocolate chip cookie recipe that is so sweet it almost makes my teeth hurt."

"That sounds delicious, but Linda's only has carrot cake for dessert."

"Yes, but Tania said I make all the calls."

José's eyes sparkled, and he laughed. "She did, didn't she? I wouldn't mind a gooey cookie, that's for sure. We don't have any chocolate chips, though." José leaned forward and glanced out into the diner. "Hey, Boyd," he called. An older man in a plaid shirt looked up from his food. "Miss Ivy here is going to make some cookies, but we don't have any chocolate chips."

The man stood and rubbed a hand over his bald head. "I'm on it. I haven't had a cookie in a long time." Boyd left his burger unfinished and rushed from the diner.

"You're going to have a friend for life now," José said, grabbing a rag and wiping off the counter. It didn't look dirty, but with so little business, there probably wasn't much to do. "Boyd comes in most days. He doesn't have any family around, and he doesn't like to cook."

"Carrot cake isn't my favorite. I've always wondered why Linda doesn't give people a few choices."

José tossed the rag into the sink. "Don't ask her. She gets steaming mad when anyone wants her to expand the menu. I would love to cook a variety of food, but she has a lot of rules. Our breakfast crowd would triple if she let me make bacon and eggs. My pancakes are as good as they come, but no one wants to eat them every other day."

I pulled an apron over my head and grabbed a hair net. "Every other day? I thought there was a different breakfast for each day of the week."

"There's still a different lunch and dinner, but breakfast is always pancakes or grits. We're lucky to get over five customers for breakfast on the grits days." José opened a large pantry and pointed inside. "You should be able to find the ingredients you need in here and in that fridge over there. You can use the mixer."

I entered the perfectly organized pantry and pulled out the powdered sugar and flour. "Do you see my uncle much?" I wasn't sure if I should ask. Uncle Rob was my mom's older brother and only a year younger than Aunt Linda. He was also, unfortunately, the town drunk.

José nodded. "Rob comes in for most of his meals when he feels up to eating."

I nodded and grabbed a box of butter from the fridge.

José turned the grill down. "If word gets out we're serving something besides carrot cake, we might have a rush on the diner. You better make a big batch. You also better hope word doesn't get back to Linda."

I placed all the ingredients on the large island. "Well, she's the one who begged me to come. I'm not going to sit here doing nothing all day." It came out confidently, but inside, I worried. I didn't like confrontation. If I'd thought about it a little longer, I might have changed my mind rather than go against something Linda wanted. There was no going back now. Boyd expected cookies, and I wouldn't disappoint him.

José leaned against the counter. "I'm not complaining. I have always wished that I could make more creative things. The enchiladas I bake would make your mouth water."

The butter wrapper was giving me a bit of trouble. "I wonder why Linda likes such a limited menu."

"She doesn't want to deal with buying a large variety. If people actually ordered from a menu, we would need more cooks as well, and then she would be out more money."

"But more people might come."

"True. Linda knows her mind, though."

The bell above the diner's door rang, and I glanced through the kitchen window. A man in a khaki button-up shirt with dark brown pants entered the diner. He had a star on his pocket and something on the other side that might be a nameplate. I couldn't see what it said from where I stood. That wasn't what caught my eye. He was the best-looking guy I'd seen in a long time. He looked to be in his early thirties, with brown hair and an impressive shoulder span. I turned away so I wasn't staring.

"Hey, Sheriff," José said through the window.

"Hi, José. How are the burgers today?"

"Perfect as usual."

"Can I get one?"

"Sure thing."

Livy stood by the window and waited while José put together a burger. I peeked up, but all I could see was the top of the sheriff's head. He must be sitting at the counter.

"Who does the car out front belong to?" the sheriff asked. "I've never seen it before."

My heart started pounding in a way that made little sense. It wasn't like I'd done anything wrong to attract the sheriff's attention.

"Linda's niece has come to help for a while. Come say hello, Ivy."

I wiped my hands on my apron and moved over to the window. I peered out at the sheriff and forced myself to smile. "Hi, I'm Ivy Clark."

He nodded. "I'm Jett Malone. I would guess you were related to Tania, even if I wasn't told. You have the same green eyes. It's nice to meet you."

"You too," I said, trying to keep my smile. I didn't like being compared to Tania. We have the same high cheekbones and are about five feet five, but that was where our similarities ended. I spent time exercising, and Tania refused to do anything that caused her to sweat, so my arms were toned, and hers weren't. Her short hair always looked perfect, while my long blond hair was often out of control.

Livy handed Jett his food and returned to wiping a table.

"Sheriff Malone is the best sheriff we've ever had," José told me before leaning toward the man. "You might want to stick around town for a while."

Sheriff Malone raised one eyebrow. "Oh? Is there a problem?"

"No. Ivy is making chocolate chip cookies."

The sheriff's mouth curved up. "I will definitely stick around for that. Does your aunt know?"

I shrugged. "She didn't give me a lot of direction, so I figure I can do what I want until told otherwise."

"How long until the cookies are finished?"

"I'm just starting. The first ones should take less than an hour if Boyd is fast." I turned and went back to the mixer. Sheriff Jett Malone might be the one bright lining to Muddy Creek. That wasn't true. I liked José as well. I remembered thinking he was nice the last time I visited Kansas.

José and the sheriff exchanged small talk while I returned to creaming the butter and sugars. My mouth turned down when I thought about how I must appear with my hairnet and apron. At least the apron was mostly clean. I wasn't the cleanest baker, so it probably wouldn't be long before I was covered in flour.

The dough came together nicely. I took the mixing bowl from the mixer and stirred in a liberal amount of chocolate chips by hand. With the amount of chips I put in, it was the only way. The mixer always pushed them to the bottom, and they clinked around without mixing in. I was starting to regret it. Stirring this much dough by hand was difficult. Jett mentioned Linda's name, and I stopped stirring and listened.

"You think someone tampered with her car?" José asked.

"I'm not positive," the sheriff said. "I'm not a mechanic or anything, but it looks like the brake line was cut."

"I would hate to be whoever did it. Linda won't take that sitting down."

"Don't spread it around. I might be wrong. I'm only telling you because I was hoping you would come look at it for me once you get off."

"Sure thing."

I couldn't hear what else they said because the door opened, and a loud group of teenagers entered. My heart pounded, but I would have to keep it to myself. Who would want to hurt Linda? She might not be my favorite person on the planet, so I imagined she could rub someone the wrong way, but enough to cause a car accident?

Chapter 2

I poked my head into Aunt Linda's living room. Linda sat on a green-and-tan-checkered sofa with her leg propped up on an ottoman. Her white cast started above her knee and ended at her toes. She peered over her gold-rimmed glasses and shifted her position. Her mouth was in a firm line, making it hard to know whether she was happy to see me.

"Ivy," she said. "Come sit." She motioned to a wooden rocking chair at her side. I came into the room and walked around a pile of magazines that looked like they had been tossed haphazardly into the air and left where they fell. I would have picked them up, but they were the least of the problems with the room. A half-eaten pizza from a different town was on the coffee table, along with several soda cans and wrappers. Linda had never been neat at home even though the diner was.

"It's nice to see you, Aunt Linda," I said, trying not to look at the seat of the rocking chair as I sat. I didn't want to know what might stick me to its surface.

"How did things go at the diner?"

"Fine."

"No major catastrophes?"

"Nope. It was all smooth." I hadn't seen my aunt in a long time, but she wasn't wasting time with pleasantries.

Linda ran a hand over her short, curly brown hair. "I wasn't too worried. Tania knows what she's doing."

"I thought Tania was here."

"Why would she be here? She was supposed to be at the diner all day."

I shrugged. "She only stayed for a minute after I got there. She said she was coming to take care of you."

Linda's eyes narrowed. "Hmm. She must have gotten distracted."

"I'm not really sure you need me here," I said. "I think José and Livy have it all under control."

"I need someone from the family there. You can't trust paid workers."

I wondered if that meant I wasn't getting paid. "What are you reading?" I asked, pointing at a book on her lap.

"Stupid book," she said, holding it up. "It has the most juvenile themes. It's like the author was writing for teenagers."

"It's a YA book, so you have to expect that."

She glared at me. "YA? What is YA?"

"Young adult."

"Well, I'm still giving it a two-star rating."

I pursed my lips but didn't say anything.

"Hey, Mom," Tania said, entering the room. "What's up, Ivy?"

Linda sat up tall and focused her glare on Tania. "Ivy says you didn't stay at the restaurant."

"Sure I did. I was there all day."

Linda sneered at me. "See, I told you she was there."

My mouth turned down as I looked at my cousin. "You left me there without telling me almost anything."

Linda shook her head. "No one likes a tattletale."

This coming from a woman who found young adult themes to be juvenile. I wasn't sure this was going to work out.

"I shouldn't stay at the diner while you're hurt," Tania said with a pout.

"Don't worry. That's why Ivy is here."

I forced myself to keep my arms at my side even though I wanted to cross them angrily. "Can you give me more direction? I'm not really sure what to do at the diner."

Linda sighed, and I felt like a naughty child instead of a twenty-nine-year-old woman. "You are just there to make sure everything runs smoothly. You pick out the menu for the week and make sure you order in what we need. If you need help, José knows how to put in the orders. I usually rotate through the same things. Monday's pancakes for breakfast, a chicken sandwich for lunch, and a baked potato for dinner, etcetera."

"Do you have it written somewhere?"

"No, just be creative."

Linda wasn't being very helpful, considering I was here to help her out. If I had known Tania would dump it all on me, I wouldn't have come.

Tania turned to her mom. "Uncle Rob is in the kitchen."

Linda groaned. "He better not be in my chocolate."

My eyebrow rose, and Tania grinned. "Mom makes chocolates and keeps them in a tin on top of the fridge. Uncle Rob always sneaks them when he comes over."

"I should go see him," I said, standing. I wasn't close to my uncle, but he was always nicer than Linda.

"Have you checked in at the B&B?" Linda asked.

I paused. "B&B? I thought I was staying here."

Linda and Tania both looked at me like I was growing horns.

"You don't want to stay here," Linda said. "The B&B is a lot closer to the diner."

I was panicking. "I don't have money for that."

Linda threw her hands in the air. "Well, what was your plan?"

"I thought I was staying here like I usually do."

"That was when you came for a short time. I can't have you interrupting my routine."

Tania tapped her lip. "Can't she stay in the little room above the diner?"

Linda looked put out. "I suppose. You'll have to pay a bit for rent, though."

I was normally pretty mellow, but this pushed me past my limits. "You needed me to come here! You want me to work for free every day and then pay you rent? I don't have any way to make money while I'm working for you."

"Fine," Linda grunted. "Stay there for free."

I rushed from the room before saying something I might regret. I wasn't doing this for Linda anymore, but I would stay for my mom. She would probably understand if I left, but she would worry about her sister. I made my way through a cluttered hallway and into the kitchen.

"Ivy!" Uncle Rob exclaimed when I entered. He sat at an oak table, his bottle of liquor resting in one hand. "It's been a while. I think you've grown."

I smiled. "It's been two years, and I think I was already grown then."

"You married yet?"

"Nope."

"Don't worry. Lots of folks don't get married these days."

I didn't point out that he was one of those. Rob had been engaged once, but his fiancée wouldn't tolerate his drinking. He couldn't hold a job for long and only survived because Gramma Sue had left him a monthly allowance in her will. She'd been smart enough not to give him all the money at once, or he might have drunk himself to death.

Rob stood and rubbed his overweight stomach and yawned. He tossed his bottle into a trash can and grabbed a stool from the bar. He placed it by the fridge and wobbled as he climbed to the top. His hands wrapped around a metal tin, and he unscrewed the top.

I smiled. "Is Aunt Linda okay with you snitching her chocolate?"

He grinned. "She doesn't know I do it." He stuck the chocolate in his mouth, placed a few more in his pocket, then hopped down and replaced the stool. I didn't want to think about how gross the chocolate would be by the time he pulled it out of his pocket. He glanced at his watch and squinted to read it. "I think it's about time for me to get going." He took a few unsteady steps.

"Hey, Uncle Rob? Do you want me to drive you back to your house?"

His shoulder scraped against the doorframe. "Nope. Legs are good enough for me."

I shook my head as I watched him disappear into the hall. Before I could decide my next move, Tania came into the kitchen. She opened a cupboard and scanned a row of keys hanging on hooks. She plucked one off and held it out to me.

I took it and turned it in my hand. "What's this?"

"It's to the room above the diner. It's a real dump. Sorry about that."

I stuffed the key in my pocket and shrugged. "It'll be fine."

"Did you scare Rob away?"

"No, I think he needed to get home and rest."

Tania snorted. "That man. Being related to him is an embarrassment. Everyone judges us because of him."

"Has anyone ever tried to get him some help?"

She looked at the ceiling and shook her head. "So. Many. Times. My mom yells at him at least once a month, and he just tunes her out. We try to get him to understand what he's doing to the family, but he doesn't care."

"Why did you tell your mom you were at the diner?"

Tania waved her hand as if it were nothing. "I love the diner, don't get me wrong, but that doesn't make me want to spend my entire life there. When I inherit it someday, I'm figuring out a way to make more money and hire more people. Then I'll be recognized as the owner but won't actually work there. I keep trying to convince my mom to do better with things, but she doesn't like to change what works for her."

"I think most people are like that."

"I guess."

There was no reason to stay, so I said goodbye to Linda and Tania and returned to the diner. I had seen the stairs going up to my new room, but I'd never been up there. The stairs were blocked off with a Do Not Enter sign. I moved the rope and hauled my suitcase up the stairs. When I got to the top, I stood in front of a closed door. I opened it and peered inside. I flipped on the light and gasped. The room looked like it hadn't been touched in a decade.

Sighing, I placed my suitcase on the floor and frowned. There was a layer of dust on the carpet. On. The. Carpet. I figured it used to be blue but was now a light gray. I tried not to see the spiderwebs, but they were prevalent. A desk stood against one tan wall and nothing else. No bed, nothing. The only thing that stood out as being a good thing was the window seat. I'd always wanted one. A small bathroom off to the side with a showerhead that came out of the wall and a drain underneath was a sad but necessary addition to the room. I definitely wasn't getting paid enough. And to think, my aunt wanted to charge me to stay here.

Chapter 3

I woke up the following morning to the smell of pancakes and the sound of something clanging downstairs. I jumped to my feet and glanced at my watch. 6:30 a.m. I'd stayed up late trying to free my new room of dust and spiderwebs. Thankfully, the diner had a small vacuum. It was now clogged, but my floor was clean. My shoulder hurt from sleeping on the floor. It might have been bearable with a pillow, but I'd had to use some folded-up pants under my head.

Not surprising, the shower was cold, so I scrubbed as fast as I could and got dressed. I put on a nice pair of dress pants and a blue button-up shirt. I pulled my hair into a ponytail and hurried downstairs. The dining area had more people than I expected, but it still wasn't full. José motioned to me, and I hurried into the kitchen.

"Ivy, I'm glad you're here. Livy called in sick, and Sarah's not scheduled until the afternoon. Can you serve the pancakes?"

"Of course," I said, pulling on an apron. I grabbed a serving tray with three plates of chocolate chip pancakes. "Chocolate chips?"

José grinned. "We never have this many people on a Tuesday morning. Word about your cookies got out, and we had a lot of people come in today. I had to improvise. Those pancakes go to table three."

I nodded and made my way out. I wasn't sure which table was table three, so I counted from the door over. Three people were there, so I figured it was the right one. When I walked away, a man from table two grabbed my sleeve. I looked over to see Sheriff Malone.

"Hello, Sheriff."

"Things got busy yesterday, and I wasn't able to get back for a cookie, but José brought me one. It was delicious."

I felt my cheeks heat. "Thanks, Sheriff. Let me go get you some pancakes."

"Thank you."

I rushed back to the kitchen and grabbed two more trays.

"Are you alright?" José asked. "Your face is red."

I felt my face burn three more shades. "Fine," I said, rushing the pancakes out and then coming back into the kitchen.

"The next batch will take a few minutes," José said.

"Hey, José? I talked to my aunt yesterday. She said you know how to order from the supplier."

He flipped a pancake. "I do."

"She also said I can choose the menu."

His eyebrow rose. "Did she now?"

I grinned. "Bacon and eggs tomorrow?"

"Aha! I don't have time to get that from the supplier by tomorrow, but I can pick some stuff up from the store after work." He walked to the window and called to the patrons, "Bacon and eggs tomorrow!"

A cheer came from the crowd just as the back door to the kitchen opened, and my uncle Rob stumbled in. He looked worse than yesterday. His hair was unruly, and his shirt was half untucked. He wore the same clothing that he had on last night. Sweat ran down his face and into his collar.

"What are you doing here, Uncle Rob?" I whispered. I didn't want the patrons to see him in this condition.

"I'm not feeling too good," he said. "Can't remember what I'm about this morning."

The bell rang above the front door, and I sighed. "I need to stay to help with the breakfast rush. Go to the upstairs room and rest for a minute, then I'll drive you home." He nodded, and I guided him quietly to the stairs, hoping no one noticed. I walked him up because he was swaying.

When we entered the room, he sank to the floor and closed his eyes. Before I could leave, he was snoring.

I spent the next few hours helping José and making another batch of cookies. By the time a middle-aged woman named Sarah came to help serve, it was lunchtime. I told José I needed to take Rob home and hurried upstairs. He was in the same position, the light from the window resting on him.

"Rob, I'm ready to take you home," I said. He didn't move. A chill ran down my spine, and every hair on my arms stood on end. He was so still, and he looked a little gray. "Rob? Rob?" I said louder. I kneeled at his side and shook his arm. It was like a nightmare. I grabbed his wrist to feel for a pulse. Nothing. He wasn't cold, but no heat was coming from him either.

I took the stairs three at a time, almost falling on my face before I got to the bottom. I must have made a lot of noise because everyone in the diner stared at me. "Does anyone know where Sheriff Malone is?"

"He usually walks down the main street at about this time," a woman said. I burst through the door and scanned the street. Sure enough, he was a few buildings away. Almost all of Muddy Creek's businesses were on this one block, so there probably weren't a lot of places he would be.

"Sheriff!" I yelled, running toward him. When he saw me, he began taking big steps in my direction.

"What is it?" he asked when he reached me. I must have looked a sight because his eyes were wide.

I placed my hands on my stomach. "It's my uncle Rob. He's dead."

His brows came together. "Dead? What happened?"

"I don't know! He came into the diner earlier and wasn't feeling well. I took him up to my room to lie down, and when I went back to check on him, he was dead."

"Take me to him." We both entered the diner, and he turned to a man at the first table. "Ernie, I need you to call in an ambulance. I'll be back down in a minute." The entire room fell silent. "Tell them we have a dead man."

Even though I already knew Rob was dead, hearing Jett say it made me shudder. "What if I'm wrong, and he's not really dead?"

"We'll still need an ambulance."

Sheriff Malone's long legs had him up the stairs in no time, and I lagged behind. I forced myself to move up behind him. I kept hoping he would call out that I was mistaken and Uncle Rob was fine, but he didn't. When I got into the room, the sheriff was on his knees, leaning over Rob.

"He's definitely dead," he said, glancing up at me.

I just nodded while I fidgeted with my hands from the doorway.

He stood and came near me. "Do you know what happened?"

I tried to swallow my guilt. "Rob came in this morning and said he wasn't feeling well. He was sweating and confused. I thought it was a hangover, so I told him to come up here and lie down. I should have taken him to the doctor."

"Don't do that to yourself," he said, putting a hand on my shoulder. "It's not your fault. I would have done the same thing. Besides, the closest doctor is forty miles away. I don't see any obvious reason for him to die. I'll have to make some calls. The ambulance will take a while to get here as well."

I placed a hand on my head. "I need to go tell Linda and call my mom."

"Go ahead. I'll deal with things here, but will you please come back when you're finished?"

I nodded and hurried to my car. I called my mom and put it on speakerphone as I drove to my aunt's house.

"Hi, Ivy. How's it going?" Mom asked when she answered.

"I'm fine, but something happened."

"Oh?"

"Are you home?"

"Yes, why?"

I didn't want to tell her if she was driving or something.

"It's about Uncle Rob. He's dead."

It was quiet for a moment. "What happened?"

I told her what I knew, which wasn't much.

She sniffled. "I'm sorry you had to find him."

I nodded even though she couldn't see me.

"Does Linda know?"

"Not yet. I'm on my way to her house."

"Don't blame yourself," she said. "He probably drank too much. I've always worried something like this would happen."

I pulled onto a dirt road and ended the call. Technically, I knew it wasn't my fault, but I still should have done something more than putting him upstairs. I felt like I'd swallowed a rock. Guilt was a killer. I wasn't close to my uncle at all, so it wasn't like I would miss him. I knew the mailman better than I knew him, which made me feel worse.

I pulled into the driveway and looked at the small white house. My mom and Sheriff Malone might say it wasn't my fault, but I had a feeling Aunt Linda wouldn't be as forgiving. I took off my seat belt and made my way to the front door and rapped on it.

Tania opened the door and frowned. "You're supposed to be at the diner."

I ground my teeth together. "Something happened. I need to talk to Linda." Tania just stared at me, so I pushed past her into the living room. Linda sat in the same place where I had seen her yesterday, watching a reality show. When she saw me, her brows came together, and she pushed mute on the remote.

"Who is taking care of the diner?"

"I'm sure Sheriff Malone has shut it down by now," I said.

"What? Why?"

I took a deep breath. "Uncle Rob is dead."

"Dead?" Tania asked, coming in behind me.

Linda put a hand to her chest and looked dizzy. "What happened?"

"He wasn't feeling well, so he was lying down in the upstairs room. When I went to check on him, he was dead."

Tania sat next to her mom and put a hand on her shoulder. "We all knew this would happen. You can't drink like that and live forever."

Linda covered her face with her hands and let out a loud wail. The sound caused me to jump. "Both of you leave me be!" she sobbed.

Tania jumped up, and we both hurried from the room. Tania led me to the kitchen and motioned for me to sit at the table. "It's unfortunate, but he had it coming. I don't see why my mom cares so much. I would think she would be relieved. He's been more of a leech than a brother over the years."

I narrowed my eyes as I watched Tania fill a cup with water. "I'm sure she has good memories too," I said. "He wasn't always that way."

Tania took a sip. "He has been as long as I can remember. I feel bad for Mom, but I think it will be good in the long run. You can't believe the drain he's been on our resources."

"I thought he got a monthly allowance from Gramma Sue's will."

"He does, but he runs it out as fast as he can and then he comes and eats for free at the diner. Sometimes he eats three meals a day there."

I wasn't needed here, so I stood. "I need to go back to the diner."

"Not if it's closed."

"I don't know if it is. I'm only guessing. Besides, Sheriff Malone told me to come back."

Tania glared at me. "Why would Jett want you to come back?"

"Probably because I'm the one who last saw Rob alive, and I'm the one who found him. I suppose he has questions."

"I'll go with you."

"Why?"

"Emotional support."

I wanted to laugh. Getting any type of support from Tania would be the same as getting sympathy from a brick.

Chapter 4

I wondered if it was possible to roll your eyes so many times they got stuck in your head. If so, I might be in danger. When we had gotten to the diner, it was to find Sheriff Malone had indeed closed it and sent the staff home. As soon as we got here, Tania had gone from being cynical to being a damsel in distress. She had practically thrown herself at the sheriff and cried on his sleeve about her poor, misguided uncle.

I sat at one table, waiting for Sheriff Malone to calm her down. My cousin didn't have any shame. If I were her, I would be embarrassed. She was bad-mouthing Rob one minute and claiming her heart was broken the next. The sheriff tried to console her but also searched the room as if looking for an escape.

"I'm sorry, Jett," Tania said, wiping away a tear. "I can't seem to pull myself together."

"Don't worry about it," he said, patting her shoulder. "That's what I'm here for. You might want to go into the bathroom and fix your makeup."

Tania covered her mascara-streaked face and hurried away. I hid a smile. I bet she hadn't thought things through when she began her act. I also couldn't believe the sheriff pointed it out.

Sheriff Malone came over and sat at my table. "Tania yelled at me in high school once because I didn't tell her that her mascara had run in the rain. I realize I sounded really rude just now, but I didn't want a repeat of that. She seems pretty broken up over this."

I gave a small, pitiful smile. "She seemed fine before. Seeing you must have made it more real."

"Tania is a great actress. She likes any kind of attention. How are you doing?" he asked, resting his elbows on the table and steepling his fingers under his chin.

"I'm fine," I said. "Rob and I were never close. I feel bad, but I mostly feel sad for my mom."

He nodded. "Do you know anyone who might have something against your uncle?"

I blinked twice. "Against him? Do you think he was murdered?"

He waved his hands. "No, no, I just have to ask. The ambulance will take him to Wichita, where he will have an autopsy. My bet is that it was the alcohol."

"That's what my mom thinks. He was having liver problems a year ago. I know the doctors strongly encouraged him to stop drinking. To answer your question, I don't know anyone who had anything against him."

He nodded. "I guess that's because you don't know the people he interacts with. He's gotten himself a few enemies in Muddy Creek over the past ten years."

"Oh?" I was surprised. "Even though I didn't spend a lot of time with my uncle, he always seemed nice enough."

"Drinking has really poisoned his life. It was lucky he had that monthly allowance, or he would have been homeless. I've lost track of how often I've had to arrest him for small things."

You learn something new all the time. "Like what?"

"Mostly stealing things. He never actually broke into a house, but if he finds an unlocked door, he's been known to walk in and help himself to people's food or easily accessible things."

"Why isn't he in jail?"

He sighed. "No one ever pressed charges, so he would spend one night in jail, then go free."

I tilted my head. "If no one pressed charges, they must not be his enemies."

He glanced at the bathroom, then leaned forward. "I can't prove it, but I think most of them let it go because of your aunt. Some of them were really mad when it happened, but once your aunt talked to them, they dropped it."

"I can't imagine Linda having that kind of power."

"A lot of old bachelors live around here. Linda's Diner might not be the best in the nation, but a warm meal cooked by José isn't anything to sniff at for a hardworking guy without any family."

I leaned back in my chair and frowned. "So you are saying no one pressed charges because they didn't want to be banned from the diner?"

He shrugged. "I know it sounds pathetic, but that's my guess. How did your aunt take the news?"

"She was wailing when I left."

"She always told me she was going to reform Rob. I think it broke her heart every time he did something he shouldn't."

The door to the bathroom opened, and Tania came out. Her makeup was perfect once again, and she flashed her Hollywood smile at Sheriff Malone.

"Feeling better?" he asked.

She ran a hand through her perfect hair. "Yes, thank you. I'm sorry you had to see me like that. Did you take things off Rob? If I can get his keys, I'll make sure his house is alright."

Sheriff Malone's mouth turned down. "I can't just give you his keys. Not until we figure everything out. I know Rob had a will."

Tania put her hands on her hips. "I'm sure he does, but who is he going to leave his things to? Us. He doesn't have any other family or friends. Besides, no one would want his junk, anyway."

He shrugged. "I'm not going to hand it over yet. Sorry."

Tania's eyes narrowed, and she swung her purse over her shoulder. "Ridiculous." She turned and stomped from the diner.

"Sorry about that," I said, embarrassed by my cousin's actions.

He smiled. "Tania doesn't faze me. That was mild compared to what I've been through with her. I've known her my entire life. We went to high school together. In a class of twenty people, you get to know each other really well. The only time I haven't been around her was when I went to the police academy."

I shook my head. I couldn't even imagine that few people in a graduating class. "You must like it here if you returned to be the sheriff."

"It's a good place. I had a job on the police force in Los Angeles, but I'm not really into big-city life. A medium-sized town might be nice. I only ran for sheriff here because no one else was, and my parents talked me into it."

"So no one ran against you?"

"Nope. I got it by default."

"Do you like it?" Great, I probably sounded like I was interrogating him.

"I do. It would be nice if I wasn't the only law around here, but I'm making it work."

I raised my brows. "There's no other law? No deputy or anything?"

"Nothing. No one wants to be out here. If I ever need help, I have to get people to come in from a different city."

"That sounds awful. I bet there isn't a lot of crime here, though."

He shrugged. "It's not terrible, but I keep busy."

Sirens sounded in the distance, and we both stood and looked out the window.

"Does the diner have to stay closed?" I asked. "Linda will want to know."

"It's probably fine to open it. Just keep everyone out of the upstairs room. Just for a few days."

"Including me?" I shivered at the thought of staying in the room Uncle Rob died in.

"Yes. Keep it locked."

"I don't have anywhere else to stay."

"Stay? You're staying up there?"

"Yes."

"There wasn't a bed or anything."

I bit my bottom lip. How was I supposed to respond? I didn't want the handsome sheriff to think I was destitute or anything. Linda wouldn't want me in her house, and the B&B was out of the question. The only reason I had been free to come here was because my job had phased out. I needed my savings to last until I could get another job.

The ambulance stopped in front of the diner and saved me from answering any more questions about my odd living conditions. I followed him outside and waited while he spoke to the paramedics.

Tania stood down the street talking to a small group that had gathered to watch the diner. When she saw me, she rushed over and took my arm. "Everyone is talking about Rob, and no one is surprised."

"Word must travel fast."

"Here it does. No one has anything to do but be in everyone's business. I don't know why Jett won't let me have Rob's keys."

"Why do you want them?"

"A lot of things inside his house were inherited from Gramma Sue. I don't want someone getting in there and taking them. I don't know why she left so much to him. He sold everything worth anything, but I don't want to lose the other things for sentimental reasons."

I could understand some of that. Gramma Sue had been special, but Tania and I had been young when she died. We had both gotten things to remember her by. "I'm sure it will all be worked out in the will."

Tania made a noise that was a cross between a snort and a laugh. "I bet Rob's will is all a mess. It might not even hold up. My mom said Gramma Sue's will was really weird. There are conditions and things that get passed down to other people when the first person who inherits dies."

I remembered my mom telling me Gramma Sue's will was a bit of a headache, but I never questioned why. I could guess some of it. She had given me money to attend college, which I appreciated. There had been conditions, though. There was a list of things that I could major in if I wanted the money. I ended up majoring in history and getting a job at a law firm doing data entry. There wasn't anything I wanted to do in my field. I also taught Zumba three nights a week, but that only brought in 300 dollars a month.

Ever since I was little, I'd wanted to solve mysteries. My mom blamed it on my gramma because every time I visited, we stayed up late watching *Murder She Wrote* and *Diagnosis Murder*. It made my mom nervous, so Gramma Sue's will said she wouldn't pay for any careers involving law enforcement or anything close to it.

We watched the ambulance take Rob's body away. Sheriff Malone came over to us and turned to Tania. "I just called your mom. She needs to meet the ambulance and take care of some things. Linda can't drive in her condition, so you'll have to take her. She's waiting for you."

Tania muttered something and walked over to her pink Jeep. She got in and slammed the door, reversed, then sped away. The back of her Jeep had a pink bumper sticker that said "Barbies are real. Just check me out."

"How was Linda on the phone?" I asked.

Sheriff Malone frowned. "She sounded pretty upset. I could barely understand her."

"Do you need anything from me?" I asked. When he said he didn't, I wandered down the street looking for a store that sold anything that might work for a pillow. If I ended up sleeping on the diner floor, I would need something. I would have to take some money from my meager savings.

Chapter 5

Only one store in town had mattresses, and they only had two in stock. The owner let me put a hold on one of them, so I had a few days to come up with the money. Waiting was okay since I couldn't sleep in my room anyway. It would have been nice if I could keep the tips I'd made while I helped serve. It was all split between the servers and cooks at the end of the day, and since I wasn't on the payroll, I didn't get any of it.

I had found a cheap pillow and blanket so I would be a bit more comfortable. When I was walking back to the diner, a small gray kitten came over to me and rubbed against my ankles. I held a bag with the pillow and blanket, but this kitten needed a little cuddle.

I placed my things on the sidewalk and picked up the curious little thing. I cradled him close to me and rubbed his ears. "What's your name?" I asked, listening to him purr. "You are so sweet."

"And he's a bit of a scoundrel," said a voice behind me.

I turned to see a smiling black man I'd never met before. "Is he yours?"

"Yes," he said, rubbing the kitten's head. "I'm Brian Hooper. I run the library. You must be Linda's niece."

I nodded. "I'm Ivy Clark."

"I'm sorry about Rob. Is there anything I can do?"

"Thank you. I'm not sure what will happen, so we are all right for now."

"Don't hesitate to come ask for help if you need it. I'm not just saying that."

"Thank you. So this cutie belongs to you?"

"Yep. My cat had kittens five months ago. I've found homes for all of them except this one. Are you interested?"

I ran my finger over the kitten's ear. "I wish I could keep him. I don't have any cat supplies, and it's not in my budget right now." As soon as I said it, my mind started calculating the cost of the supplies I would need. If I returned the blanket—

"If you take him, I'll give you supplies to last a month."

"I can't let you do that."

"Believe me, it's worth it. Finding good homes for cats around here isn't easy. Everyone has a mice problem, so everyone already has cats. When this litter was born, I went right out and bought a litter box, food, and a cat bed for each of them because I knew that was the only way anyone would take them."

"With a lot of mice, wouldn't people want lots of cats?"

He rubbed a hand over his head. "Well, I'm a bit of a softy. Some people will take any cat and let it run around their farms. I'm sure that's a fine life for a cat, but I want my cats to be loved. I can tell you would give him that."

Goose bumps ran across my arms, and I knew I was keeping this little fellow. "I'll take him."

Brian's smile stretched across his face. "I thought you might. He's had his shot, and he's been fixed. I have all the papers I'll bring to you. I'll gather all his things and bring them to the diner. I will warn you, though. He doesn't like to go outside. I've been bringing him out to get him used to it, but he would rather lay around all day on his fluffy bed staring out the window."

"I prefer that. I'd worry about him getting lost if he went out."

Brian rubbed the cat's head again. "I'll get all his stuff and bring it right over." He turned and jogged away before I could change my mind. Not that I would.

I grabbed my bag in one hand and kept the cat in my other arm. Linda would kill me if she found out I had a cat in the diner. Jett didn't want anyone in the top room, but I would have to make an exception for Creepers. Yes, I'd known my entire life that if I ever got a cat, I would call him Cosmic Creepers, after the cat on *Bedknobs and Broomsticks*.

I hurried to my room, ignoring the sheriff's instructions about staying out. I couldn't have a cat wandering around in the areas where people ate. I took Creepers into the bathroom and let him explore. For now, I could keep him here so he wouldn't mess up anything Jett wanted to see. I made sure the toilet was closed and there was nothing dangerous, then I went down to meet Brian.

I only had to wait five minutes when I heard a tap on the diner door. I opened it and let Brian in. His arms were full. I felt guilty accepting the brand-new cat items, but Brian looked happy to give them to me. He put them down on one of the tables.

"If you need anything, let me know. Have you ever had a cat before?"

I gave him a crooked smile. "Not a real one, but I've had plenty of make-believe cats."

He laughed. "Cats are the best pets, in my opinion. They do their own thing but let you know if they want something."

"I should be an expert. About once a year, I search for everything there is to know about having a cat, but then something always happens, and it doesn't work out."

"Well, I'm glad it will work out for you now."

"Do you want to say goodbye to Creepers?"

Brian chuckled. "He already has a name?"

I shrugged. "It's like I said. I've been preparing for this my whole life."

"I think I'll leave him to explore right now. I will be by to visit as soon as he gets settled."

"Sounds good. Where is the library? I thought this town was too small to have one."

"It's on the square, just around the corner from here. The bookmobile used to come through about once a month, but that seemed a little sad to me. I rented out the building and started my own library, so it's not run by the state or county."

"How do you keep it open? Do you charge?"

"Honestly, I have quite a bit of money. More than I know what to do with. The only thing I charge is two books a year."

My brows came together. "The cost of two books?"

"No, people donate two books a year. I figured if everyone in town donated two books every year, the library would grow pretty fast. That would be about one thousand new books a year. Of course, everyone doesn't do it. A lot of people don't use the library, and some just don't donate. I'm not a stickler about it. I want people to have access to books."

"That's a really fun idea. Do you give them any guidelines for what they donate?"

"I have a list of suggestions, but they can choose."

"Do they have to be new? I have loads of books back home my mom could send that are in good condition."

"That would be great."

I said bye to Brian and grabbed the pile of cat things and hurried up the stairs.

Creeper was sniffing around the bathroom. It was a good thing I'd cleaned it so thoroughly. I placed a fluffy cat bed on the floor and pulled off the tags. I peeled a sticker off the litter box and got it set up. Creepers poked his head into everything, trying to see what I was doing.

"You'll only have to stay in here for a few days," I told him. "We will make everything a lot more cozy once we can use the bedroom." He rubbed up against me, and I picked him up. "Are you hungry?" I could stay here forever with this sweet little thing, but I had a lot to do before bed.

Brian had included a matching set of food and water dishes so I placed them next to each other and filled them. I put Creepers down and watched him sniff the food.

I really should make some cinnamon rolls for tomorrow. They always taste better fresh, but I wouldn't have time tomorrow. I wished Creepers could come down into the kitchen with me, but no one wanted an animal walking around in a place serving them food. I left him to his dinner and went to the kitchen.

I grabbed the mixer and pushed down the guilt I was feeling for being so excited on the day Rob died. I told myself it was alright. I was giving Creepers a chance to have a loving home and I could be happy about that. I couldn't choose when something like this happened.

While I was baking, I ran upstairs every five minutes to check on Creepers. Each time we had a cuddle, then I went back down. I hoped it didn't ruin the cinnamon rolls. I needed to figure out a way to make enough money to pay for my new mattress and to get some toys for Creepers. It was too bad Linda wasn't paying me anything. Even a little would help.

I thought about all the books I could donate to the library. I never get rid of books, so I have a lot from my childhood. My mom keeps telling me it's time to get rid of some, and she's probably right. I'm never going to read them again. I'm just keeping them around for sentimental reasons. I'd been through a lot of series as a tween, and I liked to have my own copies. I would babysit to get money for books, and I had quite the collection. Book orders had definitely made money on me.

A meowing from above caused me to leave the rolls once more. I wasn't going to let my new friend feel lonely.

Chapter 6

The brownies smelled delicious. I placed them on the counter at Linda's Diner and inhaled. It was good I made four pans because they would be popular. It had been a few days since Rob had died, and the diner had been packed ever since. José said they never got groups as large as we had the past three days. He said it was the food the two of us ordered combined with my desserts, but I think a lot of it was because people wanted to gossip about Rob.

"I better taste test those brownies before we serve them to the public," José said.

I raised my eyebrow. "They will burn your mouth if you eat them now."

"I can wait," he said, looking into the pan. "I'll give them ten minutes."

I shook my head and grinned. "They will still be hot, but it's your taste buds on the line."

"I've burned my taste buds off for way less deserving food. I saw you grating zucchini. Did you put it in there?"

I nodded. "Zucchini brownies are the best."

"I agree. Don't tell the sheriff it has zucchini. He's against vegetables in general. If he doesn't know it's there, he'll like it. Speaking of Jett, he just walked in."

I washed my hands and turned to see the sheriff enter the kitchen. His hands were in his pockets, and his mouth was in a firm line.

"Can we help you, Sheriff?" I asked, drying my hands on a towel.

"You can call me Jett. Can I talk to you for a minute?" he asked me. "In private?"

"Sure," I said, following him out the back door. I closed it behind us and turned to face him. "What is it?"

He rubbed his lips together and looked up at the overcast sky. "I just got an email about Rob's autopsy."

I felt uneasy, but I wasn't sure why. "Was it alcohol?"

"He was definitely over any safe alcohol level. There was also an outrageous amount of opioids. Opioids plus that much liquor killed him."

I shook my head. "I didn't realize he was into drugs."

"Neither did I. I'm getting a bad feeling about the whole thing. There isn't a lot of dealing that I know of going on in Muddy Creek. I've already talked to all the people I know who have had problems in the past, and they all said they had never heard of Rob using any drugs. He couldn't get any outside of town because he doesn't drive."

I tilted my head. "Would they admit it? If they were the ones dealing the drugs, they might not want you to know."

"I thought about that. It's still not sitting right with me, though. I'm opening an investigation to see if something might be going on."

"Did you ever determine whether Linda's brake line was cut?"

He scratched his head. "How did you know about that?"

My face turned three shades of red. "I overheard you talking to José."

"I'm almost sure they were. José agrees, and he's good with cars. He used to be a mechanic until he realized he had a gift for cooking."

"So what now?"

"I'm going to have to search your room. He probably took the drug before he showed up here. From what you said, I think he just died there. After I check it all, you can go back to living there. I don't want to get a warrant. It takes too much time. Do I have your permission to search it?"

"Yes, go ahead and search. I'll be happy not to be sleeping on a diner bench."

He crossed his arms and frowned. "You've been sleeping on a bench? Why don't you stay with Linda?"

I didn't want to admit Linda didn't want me underfoot. "It's easier to be at the diner." It wasn't as bad as it could be now that I had a blanket and pillow.

We went back inside. My head was spinning. José's mouth was full, and he shrugged when I noticed a missing brownie. I smiled and shook my head.

"Those smell so good," Jett said.

"You can have one," I offered. "You might want to let them cool a bit longer."

He picked up the knife next to the pan and cut himself a piece. "They're better hot." He shoved the entire piece into his mouth, then gave me a thumbs-up.

I looked from his full mouth to José's and shook my head. "You two are ridiculous."

"That was without a doubt the best brownie I've ever tasted," said Jett.

I smiled. "It tastes even better if it's not burning your mouth."

"It wasn't that hot. So tell me, what's your secret?"

I smiled. "Zucchini."

His eyes went wide, and he looked down at the pan. "In the brownies?"

"Yes."

"You put zucchini in the brownies?"

I giggled. "Yes."

"That's the weirdest thing I've ever heard. Can I try another one?"

"Sure."

He cut another brownie and picked it up, turning it slowly in his hand. "I can't see any zucchini."

"I grate it really fine."

He took a small bite. "I can't believe it's that good. I think I've just found a new way to get my vegetables. Do you know how to make broccoli into pie or something?"

I laughed. "Nope. I hate broccoli, and I've never found a way to make it taste good enough to be worth it."

José cocked his head and looked at both of us. "Have you tried cheese or ranch?"

"Yes," I said, "and it still tasted like broccoli."

"I'll make you a broccoli and chicken casserole sometime. You too, Sheriff."

I groaned. Broccoli was the one vegetable I wouldn't touch on purpose. If José made it into something, I would have to try it to be polite.

"Do you need my key?" I asked Jett.

"I could break it open with my shoulder, but a key would be nice," he said with a wink. My stomach fluttered when I handed him the key. "Thanks," he said, leaving the kitchen.

"Oh! Jett! Wait." He turned.

"Don't open the bathroom door."

His eyes narrowed. "Okay, why?"

José grinned. "Because she's hiding a cat up there."

My head spun, and I gaped at him. "How did you know?"

"You run upstairs every thirty minutes, and I keep hearing a meow every time I'm near the vents."

Jett smiled and walked away.

The bell above the front door tinkled, and Boyd came in. He walked swiftly up to the counter and leaned over. "Hey, in the kitchen! I smelled something chocolate before I came in the door! Whatcha making in there, Ivy?"

"Brownies."

"Hey, Livy," he said, walking to a table. "Bring me at least two of those brownies before my lunch."

Livy stopped cleaning a table and laughed. "They do smell good." Her red ponytail bounced as she walked over to the window. I handed her a plate with two enormous brownies.

"What was wrong with Jett?" José asked as he kneaded some dough. "Whatever it was, the brownies seemed to cure it."

I paused, not sure what to say. Jett hadn't seemed to keep his suspicions a secret, and he'd already told José about Linda's brakes. "He thinks a mixture of alcohol and opioids caused Rob's death."

José's eyes narrowed. "Rob was the first one to admit he was a drunk. He said he would never touch drugs because he had enough problems. Does Jett think it was foul play?"

"I think he might."

The back door burst open, and Tania rushed in. "Did you hear? Jett thinks Rob might have been murdered!"

"Yeah, he's upstairs," I told her.

"He was at our house thirty minutes ago. Mom is in a fury. She thinks it's ridiculous to think anyone would kill Rob. She'd rather think he had a drug overdose. I can't follow that logic. Plenty of people have probably wanted to kill him. I know I have more times than I want to admit."

"I didn't realize he had enemies until the sheriff said something."

"He was nice when you were around. You don't visit enough to know what he was really like," she accused. I frowned. I didn't visit a lot, but Tania had never even been to Arizona, so she couldn't talk.

"Try a brownie," José said.

"Why are there brownies?" Tania asked. "Does my mom know? I'm not complaining." She scooped out a brownie and took a bite.

"She told me I was in charge and to figure it out."

"Yeah, but when she says that, she means figure out what she is thinking and do that."

"We've made a lot more money than usual," José said.

"I'm sure. I wish Mom would listen to me. This place needs more options. I won't tell her about the brownies, but I'm sure she'll figure it out eventually. She wants you to come over."

I sighed. "Right now?"

"Yes. Do you want me to take you?"

"No, I want to have my car with me."

"'Kay. I'll meet you there."

I took off my apron and hung it on a peg, then tossed my hairnet in the trash. I wondered why she wanted to see me. Maybe word had gotten back that José and I were cooking new foods. I jumped in my car and headed over. I hadn't eaten a brownie, and they might be gone by the time I returned. It was anyone's guess how many pans of brownies José, Boyd, and Jett could eat.

I pulled up to the house at the same time as Tania. We both got out and went inside. She didn't talk to me because she was texting someone. The house smelled like burnt ramen. No one would ever believe Linda ran a neat diner if they came here. She was lucky she had José.

"Come in here!" Linda called. We went in and sat in the messy room. "Did Tania fill you in?"

"About the opioids?" I asked.

"Yes."

"She did."

"My poor brother's life was such a mess. Now Jett is trying to make him sound like some undesirable character."

Tania looked up from her phone. "He was an undesirable character."

Linda gave her daughter the stink eye. "Perhaps, but he wasn't someone a person would want to murder."

Tania shrugged. "I disagree."

"How would someone force him to take drugs?" Linda asked. "He's grown and made his own choices."

I didn't feel qualified to join in the argument. I didn't know Uncle Rob the way they did.

"What are we going to do about the funeral?" I asked.

Linda waved a hand in dismissal. "Rob didn't want a funeral. He wanted to be cremated and have his ashes dumped in the creek."

I wrinkled my nose. "Are you sure?"

"Positive. You can ask your mom if you don't believe me."

"I believe you. The creek just sounds like a sad place to end up."

Tania looked back at her phone. "At least there is water in it this year."

Chapter 7

J ett didn't come into the diner for the next few days. Every time the bell above the door tinkled, I would look up like a silly teenager with a crush. I didn't know him well enough to have a crush on him, but he was definitely nice to look at.

José pulled a pan of steaming enchiladas from the oven. He was teaching me to make them, and I was sure the smell would bring people in. I wondered how long we could keep all the new foods a secret from Linda.

"Look at these and tell me they aren't the best-looking enchiladas you've ever seen," José declared, putting the pan on the counter in front of me.

"They do look good. And they smell excellent. Is it a family recipe?"

"Nah. My grandma was from Mexico and made delicious food. My mom hated to cook, so we lost all her recipes. I've never even been to Mexico. I figured these out on my own after a lot of trial and error."

"You've never been? You should go."

"I don't even speak Spanish. I took one semester in middle school and got a C. Sometimes I wonder if my enchiladas aren't authentic at all, but at least they taste great."

"I believe it."

I rubbed my lips together. They felt a little dry. Kansas must be more humid than Arizona because I usually used ChapStick several times a day. I hadn't used it since I got here, which was surprising. A ChapStick was in every bag I owned, and I usually had one in my pocket. I went over to grab my purse from the corner.

I rummaged through my bag. "What else do you like to make?"

"I make an awesome cheesy potato bake."

My hand closed over something that felt like a cylinder, and I pulled it out. It was a prescription bottle. I frowned. I couldn't remember the last time I'd needed a prescription. The label was ripped, but the part that was there said oxycodone. I turned the bottle around a few times. It was empty.

"What's wrong over there?" José asked.

"What's oxycodone?"

"It's an opioid for pain. Why?"

I held up the bottle and showed it to him. "I found this in my purse."

José walked over to me, frowning. "And it's not yours?"

"No, I've never seen it before."

"This isn't good."

My heart started pounding. This wasn't good at all. "What do I do?"

José shook his head and pursed his lips. "Don't mess around. Go straight to the sheriff."

I put a hand to my head. "But he might think I used it to kill Rob!"

"Jett's a smart kid. Go show him. Actually, wait. He almost always comes for lunch. That's in about ten minutes."

"I can't just sit here, or I'm going to have a panic attack." I went out into the lobby and passed Larry, the part-time cook. I didn't even say hello. I just rushed through the door, almost running right into Jett.

"Whoa," he said. "Where's the fire?"

"I need to talk to you." I grabbed his arm and pulled him over to the side of the diner.

"What is it?"

I held up the bottle. "I just found this in my purse."

He frowned and pulled a small ziplock bag from his pocket. He opened it and held it out to me. "Put it in there."

I dropped it in. "You just keep baggies in your pocket?"

He held up the baggy and studied the pill bottle. "Yep."

I put a hand to my stomach. "I don't know how it got there."

"I believe you. Someone might have planted it on you. Where has your purse been in the past few days?"

"I keep it in the corner of the kitchen or locked in my car. It's been upstairs and at my aunt's house. I actually left it at the grocery store counter yesterday. I remembered when I got to the car, though, so it wasn't there for long."

He grabbed his phone and typed in some notes. "I'm going to send this in for fingerprinting to see if there are any prints besides yours."

"What if there aren't?"

"Then we deal with that if it happens."

"How long does it take?"

"It depends on how busy the forensic people are. I'll have to drive it into the city. I'll do it first thing tomorrow."

I had the urge to chew on my fingernail, but I hadn't had that habit since I was a kid, so I resisted. "Why would someone try to frame me?"

"I'm not sure. Can I look in your car?"

"Sure," I said, following him to my little red car. I pulled my key fob from my purse and unlocked it. I stood with my arms folded while he looked around the seats. It wouldn't take long. I keep my car spotless.

He shut the car doors and opened the hatchback. He glanced at me. "What do you have in here?"

"Just a jack," I said, joining him. I glanced inside to find a clipping tool of some type. My mouth turned down. "What is that? A tree trimmer?" It still had a price tag on it.

He grabbed another baggie from his pocket and put it over his hand. He picked up the tool and examined it. "Bolt cutters."

My forehead scrunched. "Bolt cutters?"

"I bet if we look into it, they will be what cut Linda's brake line."

I sucked in a breath. "Who is trying to do this to me? I wasn't even in this state when that happened!"

"I'll take this tomorrow when I take the pill bottle. I don't think you should stay alone in the diner at night."

"Why? If someone is trying to place the blame on me, I shouldn't be in danger. They need their scapegoat."

"That's probably true, but it's dangerous."

"I don't have anywhere else to go. I'll be fine."

"This confirms that Rob was murdered in my mind. If it was his own doing, these things wouldn't have been planted. Why don't you go back to the diner and I'll take these things and lock them in my office? I'll come back, and we can talk some more."

I meandered back into the diner, my thoughts going a million miles an hour. Why would someone do this? My guess was that it was because I was the last one to see Rob alive. I was the obvious mark. I was also from out of town, so I didn't have any friends to stick up for me. I had Linda and Tania, but it was hard to know whether they would be on my side. I assumed they would since I had not been in town when Linda had her accident.

The diner was filling up, thanks to José's enchiladas. The part-time cook, Larry, had agreed to stay longer since things were so busy, and so had Sarah, Livy, and Kate, the servers. Everyone looked busy, and the sound in the diner was muted in my ears. My thoughts were so loud. I returned to the kitchen to see if I was needed.

"Did you talk to Jett?" José asked.

I nodded.

Boyd was in the kitchen, stuffing a cookie in his mouth. His plaid shirt was untucked, and the little hair he had was poking up. "José told me what happened. Don't worry. No one will believe you are a murderer."

"Shhhh!" I shushed, looking over at Larry. Larry was about thirty, with shoulder-length hair and an ear covered in earrings. He had earbuds in and probably hadn't heard Boyd. I glared at José. "You don't have to tell everyone!"

José chopped an onion and shrugged. "Boyd won't tell anyone."

"Nope, I won't," Boyd said. "You don't need to worry. That pill bottle could be for anything. They aren't going to tie it to you without more evidence."

I took a deep breath and felt like I might be sick. "I gave it to the sheriff. He asked if he could see in my car, and he found some bolt cutters."

José's eyes widened, and Boyd's forehead scrunched up. "Does that mean something?"

"The sheriff thinks they might be the thing someone used to cut the brake line of Linda's car."

José's face relaxed. "That's a good thing, in my opinion."

I threw my hands in the air. "How is that a good thing? That means I have two things against me."

"No, it means someone is trying too hard. You weren't even in town when Linda crashed. It couldn't have been you."

I grabbed the mixing bowl. I needed to bake something to take my mind off all this.

"Too bad the sheriff doesn't have many resources," Boyd said, scratching his stomach. "He's a good lawman but doesn't have a lot to work with."

José tossed the onions into his bowl. "That's true. And the bigger cities aren't easy to work with. They have a lot going on and don't want to get involved over here."

Their words weren't making me feel better.

The back door opened, and Tania entered. She was wearing a cute green knee-length dress and ankle boots. "Hey, all. It smells great in here, José. It's too bad Mom will eventually find out you are cooking new things and make you stop."

José shrugged. "She might change her mind when she sees how much more money we've been making. We would make even more if we had options."

Tania pulled out her lip gloss and smeared it over her lips. "You don't have to tell me. That woman is as stubborn as anything. Hey, Ivy? I'm going into Wichita, and I don't want my mom bugging me. I'm going to accidentally drop my phone in here so she can't call me. Will you make sure it doesn't get stolen or anything?"

My mouth turned down. "That's a long way to drive without your phone."

She grinned. "I'm meeting a guy I've been talking to online. If you see Jett, let him know."

I raised my brows. "Why?"

Her grin slipped away, and she rolled her eyes. "Because I want him to know I'm driving to the city to meet a guy who isn't him. It might finally kick him into gear and make him ask me out. I know he wants to. I never should have dumped him in high school."

Tania dated Jett? I thought the day couldn't get worse, but it just did. Tania made a show of dropping her phone on the floor and walked out.

"I say we toss it in the trash," Boyd suggested. "Tania has always been a little too big for her britches."

I scooped up the phone and put it in a drawer. "I don't want to buy her a new one if she can't find it." Drama wasn't something I needed more of. I wondered if the sheriff really thought I was innocent. He said he did, but he had only known me for a few days. That wasn't enough to make a character judgment call. What if, deep inside, he thought I was guilty? It definitely looked like I was.

I placed the mixing bowl on its stand. I wanted to make rolls, but I wasn't sure I had it in me anymore. Besides, rolls didn't really go with enchiladas. I felt defeated. There had to be a way to be helpful. I stretched my back. I also needed to make some money so I could pay for the mattress and have it delivered.

"Are there any exercise classes in town?"

José shook his head. "Not that I've ever heard of."

"I wonder if I could get anyone to come if I started a Zumba class."

Boyd leaned against the counter. "What's a Zumba?"

"It's a type of dance exercise. I used to teach it back home."

Boyd looked thoughtful. "We could spread the word. I'm sure there would be some interest."

"I'm not sure where I could do it, though."

José pulled a pan from the oven. "A small dance studio just down the street has been for rent for about five years. Someone tried to teach kids dance classes, but it only lasted a few months before they gave up."

My shoulders slumped. "I don't have the money to rent anything."

"It's been empty for so long they might let you rent it for a percentage of your profit. I'll talk to Mr. Everett. He's the owner."

"And I'll talk to everyone who might be interested," Boyd said. "I'd like it if you fell in love with Muddy Creek. Cookies like the ones you bake don't grow on trees, ya know?"

I smiled, but I wasn't feeling it. I doubted anyone would rent me a place for the small amount I could make. I might not be able to make anything. Who would want to take a class from someone who might be a murderer?

Chapter 8

My room might still lack what most would call necessities, but it was better than it had been. My blanket was folded on the floor next to Creepers's fluffy bed. During the day, I put the cat bed on the wide windowsill because Creepers liked to stare outside. Once a day, I tried to take him outside for some supervised playtime, but Brian had been right. He really didn't like it.

"We should go by the library," I told Creepers. "Do you want to go see Brian?" He meowed, which I took as a yes. I scooped him up and carried him downstairs. I used to read at least one book a week, but I hadn't read anything since I came to Muddy Creek.

I had to ask someone for directions and found that the library was only a three-minute walk from the diner. Most things on the square were, which made them convenient.

The library had an old-fashioned carved sign that said "Muddy Creek's Lovely Library."

Bringing a cat to the library might not be the best idea. I hadn't thought about that. I would just hurry in, say a quick hello, and see if I could borrow a book. I entered, and my mouth dropped. The library was adorable. I'd expected a small room with a few bookcases, but this library was as good as any I'd ever seen.

The building wasn't huge, but it was big enough to have several sections with signs for adult, young adult, middle grade, and children's. The bookshelves were all wood and had intricate patterns of leaves and flowers carved into the tops and edges. Large framed pictures of popular books covered the walls, and a vase of flowers brightened the front desk.

"Miss Clark and Creepers!" Brian exclaimed, coming out from behind the desk. He stuck a bookmark in the book he had been reading and came toward us. "It's good to see you."

"I probably shouldn't have brought Creepers in."

He took Creepers from me and rubbed his head. "No, it's good to see him. His mama is here somewhere."

"You let cats in the library?"

"It's like I told you. Mice. People would rather see a cat in a place of business than a mouse."

Creepers twisted around, trying to get down. Brian let him down, and he went running.

"I hope he doesn't get lost."

"He's fine. I used to bring him here. He'll just go curl up by the window."

"He does seem to like windows."

"Did you want to borrow a book?"

I nodded. "Can I? My mom is mailing all my old *Babysitters Club* books, but they haven't arrived yet."

He handed me an iPad. "Just fill out this form, and I'll get you a card."

I hurried and entered all my information, then I walked around, studying the books. I wanted something that could take my mind off my troubles. The books weren't separated by genre, so I had to look through everything. I finally settled on an Agatha Christie book and another one that was written by an author I'd never read.

"Good choices," Brian said when I handed them to him. He scanned them and printed me a reminder receipt. "There isn't a due date. I just ask people not to lose them. You will get an email if someone puts a hold on it."

"Great, thanks. Now I need to find Creepers."

Brian gestured for me to follow him. "He has a favorite window." We walked around a corner, and sure enough, he sat in the window, staring outside. A gray-and-black cat slept in the window next to it.

"Is that Creeper's mom?"

"Yeah, that's Paisley."

"It looks like she likes windows, too."

"Yep. Some people have lap cats, and I have window cats."

I smiled. "Thanks for letting us in."

"Anytime."

I picked up Creepers, and we went back to the diner. Today had been a slow day at the diner, so José didn't need my help. There was only one table with people when I came in, so I hurried up the stairs and sat on the window seat. Creepers curled up on my lap, and I opened my book. This was just like the daydream I used to have as a teenager. Sitting in the window with my cat, book, and hot chocolate. I didn't have the hot chocolate, but that could happen on a different day.

After reading for a few minutes, I realized I hadn't taken anything in. My mind had wandered back to Uncle Rob's murder. I frowned and flipped back to the first page. Creepers yawned, and I rubbed his head.

I started the page again and eventually got sucked in. Creepers fell asleep on my lap, and I kept reading. I kicked off my shoes, then pulled my feet up onto the window seat and leaned against the wall. The diner didn't sound loud below, so I didn't bother going down to help.

Time had no meaning when I was reading. Before I knew it, the sky outside was dark, and no sounds came from the diner. I looked at the clock and frowned. Even José would be gone. I should have helped clean up.

I placed Creepers on his bed and went down to see if everything was locked up. It was. I wasn't surprised. José was great. Linda was lucky to have him. I devoured a piece of bread since I missed dinner and went back up the stairs.

My reading time refreshed me, and I was ready to take on tomorrow. I brushed my teeth and got ready for bed. I climbed under my blanket and waited for Creepers. Even if he was dead asleep, he seemed to sense the moment I lay on the floor and would come sleep on me. I'd tried getting him to sleep next to me, but he liked to be on my face. I'd pull him down, and he would eventually settle for my stomach.

Chapter 9

Two days later, I sat in Linda's living room. Sheriff Malone sat on a fold-up chair, and I avoided his somber gaze. When he told me he needed to speak to me at Linda's, I figured it wasn't good.

"Spit it out, Sheriff," Linda said. "You obviously have something to say. Is it about the things you found on Ivy?"

She made it sound like I'd been hiding them.

He nodded. "The only fingerprints on the pill bottle were Ivy's. There weren't any prints on the bolt cutters, but there was brake fluid. I don't really think it will be a problem. We know Ivy wasn't in Kansas when you had your crash. We just need to have an alibi, and then we can cross her off the list."

I swallowed and looked at my hands. "The week of the accident, I was sick. I didn't even leave the house. My mom and dad had been on a cruise with spotty internet so I didn't speak to either of them. I'd pretty much stayed on the couch watching mindless TV." It sounded lame, even to me.

"Oh dear," Linda said, fanning herself with a magazine.

"You know I wasn't here," I told her. "It will work out."

"I'm sure it will," Jett said. Sometimes I thought of him as Jett and sometimes Sheriff Malone. My mind couldn't seem to decide what I should call him.

"Have you talked to Tania about this?" Linda asked.

"No."

"Oh dear."

I sighed. "Oh dear, what?"

Linda slumped back. "It's probably nothing."

Jett frowned. "If you have anything to say, please do."

"I just worry about what Tania might say when she hears this."

"Why?"

"Well, you see, the thing is...oh dear."

I wanted to scream. I was dying inside. I needed to get cleared before I went crazy.

"The day of my accident, Tania came home from the store. She said she saw a woman who wasn't from Muddy Creek. She said she would have thought it was Ivy if she hadn't known any better."

I ground my teeth so hard I was lucky they didn't crack. "I wasn't here."

"It looks bad to me."

I felt a chill run down my spine, but at the same time, I was sweating. "Why would I try to kill you? Why would I kill Rob? I have no reason!"

"Perhaps because of the will."

Sheriff Malone leaned forward. "What will?"

"My mother's."

"I've never even seen Grammy Sue's will! The only part that was read to me was the part about her paying for my college and leaving me some knickknacks."

"Who has the will?" he asked. "John?"

"Yes," Linda said. "He's our family lawyer. Would you like me to tell you about the will?"

The sheriff shook his head. "I want to hear it from John. It's his day in town, so we might be able to catch him. Ivy, will you come with me?"

I nodded and got to my feet. This was a nightmare. I followed him out of the room, trying to tune out Linda muttering, "I never would have suspected." How could she think I was behind this? Why hadn't I ordered takeout when I was sick? That would have given me an alibi. We walked over to the black Honda truck that said Sheriff on the door.

"Climb in," he said. I walked to the passenger side and got in. I felt numb. I couldn't think of a single thing that would prove I hadn't been here. My phone tracker would show my phone had been in Arizona, but that didn't mean I was with it. I buckled my seat belt and sighed.

Jett climbed into the driver's seat and turned to me. "You look pale. Don't worry. I still believe you."

"Why? It looks bad."

"It does, but it will work out. I have a feeling about it. I'm sure we can prove you weren't there. I can have someone look at your credit and debit card statements. That will show you didn't buy gas or anything in Kansas."

"But a person could use cash."

"Every gas station is going to have cameras. We can have them checked if it comes down to it, but I don't think we'll need to."

He backed out of the driveway, and I tried to tell myself it was fine, but we were going on a feeling.

"Have you met John Piper?" he asked as he drove down the dirt road.

"Yes, just the time he told me what Gramma Sue left me. I was young."

"So you have no idea what Linda was referring to?"

"No."

"Do you know anyone who would want to kill your aunt and uncle?"

I let out a slow breath, and I thought about Tania and some of her comments. I didn't want to throw my cousin under the bus, but if she was guilty... "Tania said more than once that she wanted to kill Rob. She also said he was an embarrassment to the family. I don't think she would hurt her mom, though. I figure she didn't really mean she wanted to kill him. It was just something she said."

"Do you know when she'll be back?"

"No. She's been gone for two days and didn't take her phone."

"That seems a little suspicious. I need to talk to her."

I tilted my head. "Do you think that's a good idea? I mean, should you be investigating her when you dated?"

He laughed. "Dated? What are you talking about?"

I looked over at him and ignored his gorgeous smile. "She said you dated in high school but broke up."

He shook his head, his eyes still on the road. "We went on one date our senior year. It was a girl's choice dance, and she asked me. The next day, she called me and gave me a big speech about how it would never work between us. It's the only time someone I wasn't dating has ever broken up with me."

For some reason, that lifted my spirits. "It's always hard to know when Tania is exaggerating."

"That's for sure. I didn't even want to go with her to the dance. It was in another town and had people from three schools. Big social events aren't my thing, but my mom told me it would be rude to say no. Hey, I heard you're starting a Zumba class."

I nodded. "It looks like it. At least if I don't end up in jail. The owner of the little studio in town said I could use it for free for the next two months, and then I can pay him a percent. Boyd has been telling everyone. I'm not sure if anyone will come, though."

"People will come. There isn't a lot to do in Muddy Creek, and any excuse to be social will draw people. And you aren't going to jail. We'll figure this out."

I leaned back in my seat and watched the scenery pass by. There wasn't much to see—only trees and a lot of nothing. I wondered if I would ever get used to being in a place with no mountains. We sat in silence for the rest of the drive. We pulled up to the main street, and Jett parked the truck in front of a thin brown brick building with John Piper's name and a list of his services.

We entered the building, and a woman invited us to sit in a small waiting room. "I'm surprised there is a lawyer in this place. It doesn't seem big enough. There isn't even a doctor in town."

Jett leaned back and crossed his ankles. "John grew up in Muddy Creek. He spends most of his time in Wichita but keeps this place open one day a week."

"It doesn't seem like he would make enough money for it to be worth it."

"His family owns this building, so I don't think he cares much about the money. He doesn't get much business here, but everyone in town uses him because they know him and don't easily trust outsiders."

A moment later, the woman led us to an office where a man with short brown-and-gray hair and round glasses sat behind a large mahogany desk.

"Hello, Sheriff," he said. "Who is your friend?"

"This is Ivy Clark. She's Linda Hanson's niece."

"Oh, of course," he said, shaking my hand. "Good to see you again. It's been a long time."

I only nodded. I felt ridiculously nervous, and I was afraid my voice would shake if I spoke.

"Sit down," he said. "What can I do for you?"

We sat in matching blue padded chairs. "Would you happen to have a copy of Sue Jensen's will?"

He shook his head. "Not here. I have it at my Wichita office."

"Do you remember the contents of the will?"

"A lot of it, yes. Sue made it all so convoluted and weird. I assume this has something to do with Rob's murder?"

He nodded. "Can you tell me anything involving Ivy?"

"Most of it, Miss Clark probably knows. She was given money for her education. There were conditions she met, and her college was paid for. Then there was the diner."

"The diner has nothing to do with me," I said.

Mr. Piper pursed his lips, and I felt my heart pounding. I wasn't sure if he was pausing for a really long time, or if it just felt long because I was nervous.

"The diner was a bit of a mess in the will. I tried to tell Sue she should do it differently, but she wouldn't.

The diner went to Linda, but she had no say over what happened to it after her death."

"Tania inherits it," I said, remembering her telling me the things she would do once it was hers.

"No. After Linda dies, it was to go to Rob. Next would be Ivy's mother, Candy, but Candy didn't want it, so Sue stated it would go to Ivy. After Ivy would be Tania. If Tania ended up with it, she would have the final say in what happened. Of course all the money the diner makes goes to whoever is running it at the time. They can do whatever they want with it."

My mouth turned down. "That doesn't make sense. It should go to Tania. She's worked there all her life."

Mr. Piper shrugged. "It was odd, but those were Sue's wishes. She also stated that it couldn't be sold without the permission of all parties, and if it was sold, the money would be split by everyone in the family."

"Is that everything involving the diner?" Jett asked.

"Yes, I believe so. I can copy the will once I go to Wichita next week, and I'll email it to you."

Jett stood and shook the man's hand. "Thank you."

"There is another thing," Mr. Piper said. "I was going to call all of Rob's relatives and do a will reading later this week, but since so many things are going on, perhaps I should let you know your involvement with his will."

I took a deep breath, ready for anything. "Alright."

He stood and opened a tall filing cabinet. Reaching in, he pulled out an envelope and handed it to me. My name was written in sloppy writing. My hands were shaking for no good reason. I was letting everything rattle me.

"Rob's will is probably going to be worse than your grandma's. He didn't want to deal with making decisions, so his will states that everything goes to you, Miss Clark, and you have the privilege of dividing up his assets in any way you see fit."

I was sure my face lost all color. "Do Linda and Tania know?"

"Not yet. Not unless Rob told them. That also includes his monthly allowance, which still has enough money to last for twenty years."

I must have gotten up because the next thing I knew, I was walking down the sidewalk, with Jett at my side. I had a spare key to Rob's house clutched in one hand.

"This doesn't make sense," I said. "I don't know why my gramma would do this. Tania should get the diner. I never spent a lot of time here, and she's a bit older. As soon as she gets back, I'll let her know I don't want any part of it. And Rob's will? What was he thinking? This will make everyone angry."

Jett had his mouth pressed in a tight line, and his eyebrows were crunched together.

"What is it?" I asked.

"Tania is at the top of my list of who I think killed Rob at the moment. She lied about you being here during the accident, and she's the one who has everything to gain from Rob's death. If she can place the blame on you, that gets you out of the way as well."

"I thought it might be her on the way here, but now I'm not sure. I don't think she knows how the will works any more than I did. She was talking about what she would do when she inherited the diner."

"Maybe she only spoke that way to throw you off. She might know you didn't know."

We had stopped and were standing in front of an empty shop. I crossed my arms and bit my lip. I wasn't even sure what I thought. "Are there any other suspects?"

"Yes, but I can't say who they are."

"Why not? You've told me plenty."

"But only things that involve you."

"Doesn't it all involve me? Someone is trying to frame me."

"Yes, but you are also a suspect."

I felt my face and neck heat.

"I don't think you did it, but for the investigation's sake, I have to have you on the list. You understand, right?"

I nodded my head, even though I was seething inside. I shouldn't blame him. He was only doing his job, and he really didn't know me well.

"I need to get to the diner." I turned and rushed away, not turning around to see if he was watching me. I trusted the sheriff to do his job, but this was my life at stake. I was going to solve this murder and clear my name, and I was going to start by busting into Tania's phone.

Chapter 10

Music blasted through the dance studio, and I tried not to giggle as I watched my class follow my Zumba moves. Boyd had been good to his word, and I had thirty people crammed into the small studio. Most of them were over seventy and must be Boyd's lady friends. The only man there was Boyd, and he was scrunching his forehead as he threw his arms wildly in the air. I was trying to modify my moves so we wouldn't have anyone dropping over or breaking anything.

I didn't know if it was a rule in Zumba, but when I was certified, my teacher demanded we smile at all times. It was not a natural look for me, so I sometimes wondered if I looked creepy in front of the class. Sweat rolled over my forehead, and I was surprised at how carefree I felt. Exercise really worked wonders for my mental well-being.

I tried not to look at my purse, which now held a little over a thousand dollars. I was charging thirty-five dollars a month for morning workouts three times a week. It was low, but I wasn't greedy. The first thing I was going to do was go back to the store and get a mattress.

When I turned off the music, a few people leaned tiredly against the wall. None of them had been doing it right, but that is one thing I like about Zumba. As long as you moved to the music, you got a good workout. Some of these women had hardly moved, but they weren't used to it, and they were a little old.

"Nice workout!" a woman in tight pink workout clothes said. Her light pink hair was pulled back into a tight ponytail. I think her name was Barbra, and she had to be seventy-five at least. She had been one of the better movers. She must work out regularly to keep up the way she did.

"Thank you," I said, using a small towel to wipe the sweat from my face. "I'm glad you all came."

"We wouldn't miss it!" another woman said. "It isn't every day you get to do a workout with a felon."

Barbra threw her towel at the woman. "Don't go judging, Opal. She hasn't been charged."

"And she won't," Boyd said. He was sweating more than anyone else in the room. I tried not to smile at his short shorts and knee-high socks. "She didn't do it, and the sheriff will prove it."

"How do you know she didn't?" Opal asked. "I heard she had the murder weapon with her."

"It wasn't a weapon," someone else said. "It was drugs."

"No, it was an empty pill bottle," another argued.

"Sounds guilty to me," Opal said.

I opened my mouth to speak, but nothing came out.

"I bet it was Sally Peterson," another person chimed in. "Sally has been hating on Rob for years. She doesn't care for Linda either."

Sally Peterson. I was going to file that name into my memory.

"Alright, everyone out," Boyd said, waving his arms. "We will see you all on Wednesday!"

"You gonna walk me to the diner, Boyd?" Barbra asked. "I hear there are cookies again today."

Boyd's face turned pink, and I turned away and smiled. I listened to him give an excuse, and within a few minutes, the room was clear of everyone but Boyd.

"Who is Sally Peterson?" I asked, grabbing my bag.

"You don't want to mess with Sally," Boyd said, pulling on his tank top. "You won't ever see her in the diner because Janie was right. She hated Rob and Linda. She dated Rob about twenty years ago."

I nodded as we walked to the door. "I knew he was engaged once."

"That wasn't to Sally. They just dated for a month or two. They were terrible together. She drinks just about as much as he did. According to her, Rob stole a bunch of stuff from her house one night when she was passed-out drunk. Rob denied it, and there was never any proof one way or the other. Linda told everyone Sally made it up to try to get money out of Rob.”

“Why retaliate this much later? Twenty years is a long time.”

“Don’t know. I heard the two of them had a big fight right in the middle of the grocery store about two weeks ago.”

“Where could I find her?” I asked, pushing open the door and holding it while Boyd exited.

He chuckled. “You wanna find Sally? I’m not sure that’s the best idea. She’s retired and lives about two miles from the town square. I really don’t think she could cut Linda’s brake line. She’s got arthritis in both her hands and doesn’t move around very well.”

I wasn’t going to let that stop me. She could have an accomplice or something. Tania was still at the top of my list, but I didn’t want to narrow my vision and miss the murderer.

“You have a scary look in your eyes,” Boyd said. “Don’t go doing anything you shouldn’t.”

“I won’t. Can you tell me where Rob lived? I’ve never been there, and I need to go through his things.”

“I’ll take you there later today when you are done at the diner.” He shot me an enormous smile. “By take you, I mean I'll ride with you in your car and point you in the right direction. I don't drive unless I absolutely have to."

No other solution came to me, so I went to my room and showered. I couldn't ask Linda or Tania where it was because then they would wonder why I was going there. I couldn't ask Tania anyway because she still wasn't back from Wichita. I wanted to see inside so I knew what I was dealing with.

I had already decided to split Rob's allowance equally between Linda, Tania, my mom, and me. That seemed fair, and no one could complain it wasn't. I was sure the harder thing to do would be dividing his possessions. Of course, there was a good chance all he had was junk. Tania sounded like anything of value had probably been sold a long time ago.

Time at the diner flew by, and it wasn't long before I was in the car with Boyd. Before I could back out of the parking spot, José came rushing toward us, waving his hands. I stopped and rolled down the window.

He leaned over and raised an eyebrow. "What are you two up to?"

I felt guilty even though we weren't doing anything wrong.

"We're off to search Rob's house. Wanna come?"

"Of course I want to come," José said, climbing into the back seat. I sighed. The more people involved, the more nervous I felt.

"Okay, drive south out of town," Boyd instructed.

"What are we looking for?" José asked. "Clues about his murder?"

I shook my head. "Nothing that exciting. Rob wanted me to divide his things between people, so I want to see what he had."

I saw José grin in the rearview mirror. "No pressure, huh?"

"From what Tania said, Rob didn't have a lot."

"While you look around, Boyd and I will look for clues."

"I doubt there are any. I think Sheriff Malone already searched it."

"Jett is pretty busy these days. He might not have gotten to it yet," José said.

Boyd turned around in his seat. "I'm pretty sure he was out there the other day. He came driving out this way, and there isn't a lot of reason to be out here."

"You don't even drive, but you sure get around," José said. "Why is it you know more gossip than Opal?"

Boyd laughed. "When you get to be my age, there is nothing to look forward to but gossip. And have you seen the company I keep? A bunch of gossipy old women."

"And you love it."

"I really do. I'm not sure about this new Zumbie thing Ivy's got us all doing, though."

I smiled. "Zumba."

"Right. I'll keep coming because all my friends are there, and of course I want to support Ivy, but my word. There are mirrors in the studio, and we look like a bunch of old idiots throwing ourselves around with no rhyme or reason. Turn left on the dirt road."

I grinned as I turned. "Zumba takes a while to get used to, but it's fun."

"I have a feeling if we keep it up, we might start having enough injuries to afford a doctor for the town."

José laughed. "I might have to join just to see it."

Boyd pointed ahead. "It's that old farmhouse up there."

The house didn't look old on the outside. It was bigger than Linda's house and had two stories and possibly a basement. From the looks of it, the gray siding was new, and the roof had black shingles that didn't look old at all.

"It's nice," I said, pulling into the driveway.

"Rob had the entire outside redone about three years ago," Boyd said. "It made a lot of people mad. Especially the people who think he stole from them. With the way he went through money, he shouldn't have had enough for that."

We got out of the car and walked up to the door. The door even looked new. I pushed the key into the lock, and we entered. My mouth hung open as my gaze swept over the entryway. The shiny gray tile was spotless, as was everything else. Everything looked well cared for and didn't match Uncle Rob's sloppy appearance.

José whistled. "Nice place. Who would have thought?"

Boyd scratched his head. "Not me. Of course, he never let anyone in."

We entered the living room, and I shook my head. Tania must not have ever come here. A grand piano sat in the corner, and a chandelier hung from the ceiling. We went from room to room, finding it all to be in great condition. It was also clear Rob hadn't been drinking away all of his money, or he really had been stealing from his neighbors.

The kitchen was clean but didn't have a lot in it. I sat at the small table and pulled the letter Mr. Piper had given me from my pocket. I kept putting off reading it. José and Boyd were searching through all the cupboards. I opened the letter, and my eyes scanned the paper.

Dear Ivy,

I know this is not the job you probably want, but you are the one I trust. I can't decide how to divide my things, so I want you to do it. You can keep everything or share with the rest of the family. I trust you to make a good decision. Candy could handle it, but I won't put that stress on my caring sister.

I have quite a lot of money. When Gramma Sue died, she left me with an $8000 a month allowance. I know everyone thinks I drink it all, but I don't come close. I drink cheap liquor, and I don't have needs for many things.

Everyone in town thinks I'm a thief, and I admit it's true. I don't mean to steal things, but drinking makes me stupid. I occasionally wander into houses and don't realize I've taken things. I'm too ashamed to admit it, so I bury all the things I steal in the backyard under the willow tree. It's not deep, and it should be obvious where to dig. I don't have the strength to do a good job of hiding it. If you would return the things, I would appreciate it. There is a brooch in a box that belongs to Sally Peterson.

Don't let Tania push you into giving her anything you don't want to. She might spread rumors about me selling everything, but she knows I didn't. Tania has snuck into my house more than once, but she doesn't know that I know. I'm sure she wants to get her greedy little hands on all she can. I would cut her out and not give her anything, but it's up to you.

Regards,

Uncle Rob

"What are you reading?" José asked. I stood and handed him the letter. I walked over to a large picture window and stared out at the flat land in front of me. Rob's yard didn't have many trees. There was one large willow, but it wasn't close. I wondered how much land came with the house.

"My word," José said. "I guess we need to go find some shovels."

Chapter 11

I wiped the sweat from my brow. Rob had been right. It was easy to find where he had buried things. They were the places that weren't packed down. Rob might have kept his house clean, but his backyard was a mess of weeds. The yard was at least two acres, and he hadn't done much with it.

I leaned against my shovel. "What if there are things hidden under the weeds? We don't know how long he's been doing this."

José pulled a wooden box from his hole and brushed off the dirt. "I think we will have to dig up the entire area, just to be sure." We had already found several wooden boxes. Some had things like real silverware and jewelry, but some had ridiculous things like hairbrushes and melted candy bars. Most of the things we found had a sticky note attached with the name of the person he had stolen it from. At least that was what we assumed. There were a few without.

Boyd was sitting, sorting things into piles. His back had begun hurting, so I made him stop. I wondered if we should call the sheriff or if we should return everyone's things individually. I didn't know if there was a law about it.

I glanced out at the swaying miles of tall grass and wildflowers. I missed the mountains, but something about the Kansas landscape was breathtaking. The sky seemed to go forever. The wispy clouds gave us an occasional break from the sun, but I wished they were thicker.

"My legs itch," I said, scratching.

"It's the chiggers. They're terrible this time of year," Boyd said.

"What's a chigger?"

"Little biting mites. Don't you have them in Arizona?"

"I'm not sure."

"I always spray repellent if I go out in the long grass. Tania wears those funny little ankle bands dipped in lavender to keep them away. I don't know if it works, but you could ask her about it."

I scratched again. Those things were horrid. I might have to try it. I'd wondered about the colorful bands Tania wore every day, but I figured it was some style I didn't know about.

"Here's the brooch," José said, holding up a small oval piece of jewelry. I took it and turned it in my hand. It was gold with a red flower in the center. I placed it in my pocket. I would take it with me when I went to talk to Sally Peterson. "This has Sally's name as well." He handed me a gold chain, and I put it with the brooch. "Actually, everything in this box has her name."

I shook my head. "Come on, Uncle Rob. This is ridiculous."

A loud boom sounded from the house. We all turned to see smoke billowing into the air.

"Is the house on fire?" I asked as we all began running toward the house.

"I think it's in front of the house, but I'm not sure," José said. We quickly left Boyd in our dust, and I struggled to keep up with José. Who knew a middle-aged cook could run like this? We rounded the corner of the house and stopped at the sight in front of us. My car was on fire. I sank to the dirt and covered my mouth with my hands. It had taken me three years to save up enough money to buy that car with cash, and I'd had to wait over a month to get a red one.

Boyd sat down beside me and pulled his cell phone from his pocket. "I'll call the sheriff."

José grabbed the hose and sprayed the car. It was pointless. I could tell the car was a loss. I wondered if the insurance paid for cars blowing up while parked and not running. I could hear Boyd talking, but I wasn't listening to what he told Jett. There was nothing to do but wait.

It wasn't long before I heard a siren. I stood and dusted off my pants. A small red fire truck came zooming down the dirt road. "I didn't think Muddy Creek would have a fire department."

Boyd stood and nodded. "It's all volunteer."

The truck stopped in front of them, and Jett jumped out in his regular sheriff clothing.

"The sheriff is on the volunteer fire department?"

Boyd shrugged. "Someone has to be."

Another man I didn't know was with them. He had a firefighter suit but not a helmet. José backed away and let Jett and the other man extinguish the fire. It didn't take long, but they kept spraying the blackened car for a few minutes after it was out. Jett talked to the other man, who nodded and left in the fire truck.

Jett's hair was messed up, and he was a little wet, but he didn't look like a person who had just put out a fire. I shook my head. I needed to stop trying to make him invincible in my mind. José had already helped a lot with the hose before the others had come, so it hadn't taken long to extinguish.

"What happened?" he asked. We told him what we had been up to, and he frowned. I handed him the letter from Rob, and he read it. "You should have called me as soon as you read the letter."

Boyd cocked his head. "Why? Us reading the letter didn't make the car blow up."

"No, but you shouldn't have dug up the stuff without me. It could have evidence."

I felt confused. "Evidence of what? That Rob was a crook? We already knew that."

"No, I already searched the house for any evidence of his murder, but there could be something in what he buried."

"Like what? The murderer wouldn't have buried something in Rob's backyard."

Boyd chuckled. "I bet Sheriff just doesn't want us going on a treasure hunt without him."

José laughed. "I bet you're right."

Jett gave them a crooked smile, and his eyes danced. "You might be right. Can you at least show me what you found?"

"Sure, but what about my car?"

"I'm going to let it sit for a while before I snoop around. I'm sure it was done on purpose."

"If someone is trying to frame me, why blow up my car? That makes me look less suspicious."

Boyd stared at the car. "Or people might think you blew it up yourself to destroy any evidence."

I shook my head. "What evidence?"

"I dunno. Fingerprints."

"It's my car. It's going to be covered in my fingerprints."

José's eyes lit up. "Maybe they did it to cover up *their* fingerprints."

Jett drummed his fingers over his opposite arm. "I already checked for fingerprints on the car after we found the bolt cutters. There weren't any. For now, why don't you show me what you found in the back?"

We walked around back and toward the willow. Something wasn't right.

José came to a stop. "The stuff is gone."

I ran over to the tree. He was right. Everything we dug up was gone. Jett caught up to me and looked out at the miles and miles of grass, flowers, and weeds.

I pointed at the dirt. "There were a bunch of small wooden boxes here."

He ran a hand through his hair. "If someone took them and hid in the weeds, they could be anywhere. All they would have to do is lie down and finding them would be almost impossible."

Boyd shrugged. "That's true, but they would have to come out eventually, and they would be covered in chiggers and ticks. How far could they actually get? I have the patience of Job. I can sit on the back porch and stare out at the weeds to see if someone pops up."

Jett nodded. "You do that, and I'm going to go look around for a while. A spot might be trampled down if they went into the weeds."

"We can look as well," I said, motioning to José.

"Sure thing," José said. I'll start on the east side, and you start over there," he said, pointing. I went over to where he indicated and started looking through the weeds. Jett was probably right. A person could drop down where they were and make it really difficult to be seen. Still, they would have been carrying all those boxes. That couldn't be easy.

As soon as I had that thought, I saw some weeds flattened down. A foot away was some more. It could be from someone walking on them. I looked over at where the sheriff was. He and José were in completely different places, and they weren't close. I could follow the broken weeds, but I didn't want to ruin anything that might be evidence.

"Hey!" I yelled. They both turned to face me. I waved my arms, hoping they would come running. They did. I waited patiently. Boyd stood on the porch, looking over. When they got to me, I pointed at the ground. "I think they might have walked here."

Jett studied the ground and nodded. "I think you're right. It could have been an animal, though. I'll follow it. You two keep looking, just in case."

I grinned. "Sure. I find it, and you get to do the fun part."

He smiled. "It's my job. I shouldn't even have you all helping me."

He walked off into the weeds, and I turned to José. "I think I'm finished looking. That has to be where they went. Let's go wait with Boyd."

"I agree." He glanced at his watch. "This is all taking longer than I planned."

"Do you need to be somewhere?"

"Nah. I'm just a tired old guy who goes to bed early."

"You aren't *that* old. I could barely keep up with you when we were running."

"I run in the mornings. I've been doing it for years. If I'm going to spend long days standing in the kitchen, I need to get some exercise in."

We walked over to Boyd. He was still watching Jett. "Did you find anything?"

I shrugged. "We might have. Some weeds might have been walked on." The porch wasn't big, but it had three steps. I sat on the top. "I don't think this was aimed at me. Blowing up my car was probably only a distraction. We were so focused on it that they were able to take the stuff and disappear."

José sat next to me. "I bet you're right. If you are, then it might not be Rob's killer. It might be someone who wanted to get their stuff back."

Boyd remained standing on the porch, watching over the area. "Even if that's true, it could still be the killer. Rob might have stolen something from them."

José rested his elbows on his knees. "But if it was the killer and they are trying to pin it on Ivy, then it would be careless to ruin her car."

I sighed. "It seems unbelievable to think someone would know we were digging this stuff up and be ready to blow up a car. If they knew the things were buried out here, they could have come and gotten it earlier."

José nodded. "That's true."

I pulled Sally Peterson's brooch from my pocket. "Where can I find Sally Peterson? I want to go talk to her about the brooch."

"She doesn't live far," José told me. "She's probably Rob's closest neighbor."

"And they've been hating each other for twenty years? I probably would have moved."

"Being someone's closest neighbor over here doesn't mean they are actually close. I'd guess she lives about a mile farther down the road."

"Does she live alone?"

"No. Her daughter and granddaughter live with her."

"She was married before?"

José nodded. "Her husband died a few years after they were married. Her daughter is about thirty-five, so it was a long time ago."

"I don't think she did it," Boyd said. "Fifty bucks says it was Tania."

"I'm not taking that bet," I said. The more I thought about it, the more it felt like it must be her. The longer she stayed away, the more guilty she seemed in my book.

While talking, I'd completely missed the change in the sky. "Wow," I said, staring at the majestic pink, purple, and orange sky. "Now that is a sunset." I've seen a lot of beautiful sunsets, but nothing like I've seen since coming here. The vast sky makes them so large and majestic. If I were an artist, I would paint Kansas skies.

"Where did Jett go?" José asked. We all started scanning the area. Before I could panic, Jett came running over from around the corner.

His shoulders slumped. "We lost them. The footprints went out, then around to the road."

"Did they have a car waiting?"

"I don't know. I didn't see anything when we drove in."

I had a thought, and it wasn't my favorite. "How far are we from town?"

"About three miles."

"Great. That's a long walk."

"Walk?"

I tilted my head and stared at Jett. "You came in on the fire truck, and we all came in my car." I saw the moment they all understood what I was saying.

Boyd sat on the porch. "I'm too old to walk that far in the evening."

José smiled. "Only in the evening?"

"Especially in the evening."

Jett pointed at the garage. "Rob had a car. He never used it, but I remember when he bought it. He told me he was going to have someone drive it around once a week to keep it in good shape. I'd hoped it meant he might be thinking of giving up alcohol."

It didn't matter if he had a car or not. "We don't have the keys," I said.

"I'm sure they're inside."

"I saw keys hanging on a hook by the door," Boyd said, getting to his feet and opening the back door. He grabbed a key chain with three keys on it and handed it to me.

We entered the garage and found a Kia Soul. I'd seen these around and thought they might be fun. This one was dark gray. I was learning that Rob's favorite color was gray. We all got in, and I inhaled the new car smell. The car was spotless. Rob must have only gotten it for show. I looked at the keys. None of them looked like a car key. I studied the steering wheel and frowned. There was nowhere to put a key.

Jett was in the passenger seat. He turned to me. "What's wrong?"

"There's no keyhole."

"It doesn't have a keyhole. You just push this button," he said, pointing at a small round button.

My brows came together. "That's dumb. How do you keep someone from stealing it?"

José snickered from the back seat, and Boyd looked as confused as I did.

Jett gave me a half smile and grabbed the keys. He held them up and showed me the rectangular thing I thought was a key fob. "You have to have this with you. When it's in the car, you can start it."

I could feel my face turn red, but how was I supposed to know? Technology was getting tricky. I buckled my seat belt and pushed the button. Nothing happened.

Jett flashed me a gorgeous smile. "Push the brake while you push the button."

"Is there a button that makes it fly, too?" I asked as I started the car. A big screen lit up with a map on it.

Jett clicked his seat belt. "Nope. No flying."

Chapter 12

During a lull the following morning, I slipped out of the diner to go talk to Sally. I got in Rob's car and drove out of town. I really liked this car. With the push of a button, I could ask it where things were, and it would tell me. Internet was spotty around town, but it was still nice. I'd had to google how to open the gas cap, but thankfully, no one was around to see that.

Tania's phone password was beyond me. I'd tried to break into it after my shower this morning, but I didn't know where to start. After a few failed attempts, it had locked me out.

I pulled up to the first house after Rob's. It reminded me of a cottage from a storybook. It was bright yellow with white trim. The yard was full of rose bushes and lilac trees. I hopped out of the car and walked up the curvy brick walkway. I pushed down my nerves and knocked firmly on the door.

A woman with a messy brown braid peeked out. "Yes?"

I tried to give her a friendly smile. "Hello. I'm here to see Sally Peterson."

The woman narrowed her eyes. "Who are you?"

"Are you Sally Peterson?"

"No."

I kept my smile. "Then I'm not here to see you." I was sure it sounded rude, but I didn't want to explain myself to everyone. I was nervous enough as it was.

The woman's blue eyes flashed with anger, but she just turned and said, "Mother, there is someone to see you."

"Well, send them in," a woman called back.

The daughter held open the door and motioned for me to enter. I went in and followed her into a sitting room. Sally Peterson sat in a rocking chair. Her appearance surprised me. From what I'd been told, she was probably around my mother's age, but she looked a good twenty years older. Her hair was almost completely white and a little greasy, hanging to her shoulders. A girl about eight sat on a loveseat holding an iPad and twisting a piece of long brown hair around her finger. She had neon-green glasses, and she was frowning at me.

"Well, sit down and tell me who you are," Sally said, pointing at a sofa. I sat down, and Sally's daughter sat by the little girl.

I cleared my throat, and the little girl made a disgusted face. "Gross, Mom. She's spreading her germs." Her mom just stared at me.

"I'm not sick. I was clearing my throat," I said lamely. The girl turned up her nose and moved her legs so they were angled away from me.

"What do you want?" Sally asked.

"I'm Ivy Clark. Rob was my uncle."

Sally's eyes narrowed. "Why are you at my house? I don't want any of Rob's ridiculous relatives here."

"I heard you came to help after Linda's accident," the daughter said.

"Shush, Darcy," Sally said. "No one is talking to you."

Darcy put her arm over her daughter's shoulders and slumped back. Darcy didn't look a lot older than me, but she looked worn down. I wondered if Sally was the reason for that. She had bags under her eyes and looked like she hadn't slept in a while.

I turned my focus back to Sally. "I found something at Rob's house that I wanted to return to you."

She leaned forward. "Oh?"

"I guess my uncle was a bit of a thief, and I found some things I need to return to people."

"You bet he was a thief," Sally muttered, watching as I pulled the gold chain from my pocket.

"My mother's necklace! I knew he took it. The sheriff at the time said he couldn't go searching everywhere with no warrants, but I knew it was that no-good man."

"I also have this," I said, handing her the necklace and the brooch.

"Ohhh, Grandma's brooch!" She clutched them to her chest. "That rotten man. I can't believe I let Darcy go clean for him after all he put me through."

My heart sped up. "She cleaned for him?"

"Twice a week," Darcy said.

My nose was beginning to itch. Someone in here was wearing a liberal amount of perfume. "I hope you understand. I'm sorry for what my uncle put you through. I hope you will let me buy you a meal at the diner one day."

"I will not step foot in that diner as long as Linda owns it!" Sally huffed. "If there is one person in the world I hate more than Rob, it's Linda."

"May I ask why?"

"She's your aunt, right?"

I nodded.

"Then you should know her character. She spread all sorts of lies about me, and she's been doing it for years."

"Because of Rob?"

"No. Linda dated my late husband before the two of us hooked up. She never got over him dumping her for me. When I started dating Rob, she was a monster. She kept telling everyone I was manipulating him."

I covered my mouth and sneezed. The little girl's mouth opened wide, and she crossed her arms and gave me the dirtiest look I've ever seen. "She's gross, Mom," she whispered.

"Shhhh, Netty," Darcy said. The girl pressed her lips together, and her eyes shot daggers at me.

I smiled at the girl. "Netty is a pretty name."

"My name is Antonette, and I am named after a queen," she said with an arrogant sniff.

"That's nice," I said, wondering if this girl had any friends.

"It is beautiful," she said. "My mom was named after a man my nanny was in love with. That isn't beautiful at all."

Sally rolled her eyes. "For goodness' sake, girl. It was a man from a movie. You make it sound so scandalous."

"Oh, was it *Pride and Prejudice*?" I asked. I didn't really care, but I was trying to figure out a way to ask questions without looking snoopy, and I couldn't think of anything to say.

"Of course it was," Sally said, fixing me with a glare.

"I love Jane Austen."

Sally's brows came together. "Who the heck is Jane Austen?"

I swallowed. "The author who wrote *Pride and Preju-dice*."

"It was a movie, not a book."

I didn't say anything. There was no way to win here. I should probably leave instead of stalling, but I needed something. I was the worst detective I'd ever heard of.

"Did you need anything else?"

"Well, uh...We found some other things that had your name on them, but someone blew up my car, and while we were dealing with that, the stuff was all stolen."

They all stared at me. I could almost hear them blinking.

"I thought I heard a siren last night," Darcy said.

"That was the fire truck."

"Do they know who did it?" Sally asked.

"No. No leads."

Did Sally's face just relax, or was it my imagination?

"I guess the sheriff found a footprint," I lied as I watched Sally's face. We had found trampled weeds but no actual prints. Sally's expression didn't change, but Darcy's eyes sparked with something. But it could be in my head. "But it turned out to be nothing."

Sally leaned back. "I like you a lot more than your relatives. Judgy people, every single one."

"I wish you knew my mom. She's a lot more pleasant. No one can blame you for your feelings. My family can be difficult. I've had very little to do with them." I hoped she might confide something to me if I was sympathetic to her.

"I knew your mom. Candy was a good person. She was a rare one in that family. If you ask me, Rob got what he deserved, and it's too bad Linda made it through her crash so well."

"You're not the only one that feels that way. The sheriff thinks Linda's crash wasn't an accident."

Sally leaned forward and grinned. "Oh? I'm not surprised."

Darcy fiddled with her hands, and Queen Antoinette continued to glare at me.

"Her car was tampered with."

Sally grinned. "With luck, they'll do a better job next time. Does the sheriff think it was done by the same person who got Rob?"

"He doesn't know. Whoever did it is trying to frame me."

"Was it you?" she asked with a gleam in her eye. "I won't tell."

"Excuse me," Darcy said, getting up and leaving the room. That was interesting.

"No, it wasn't. I wasn't even in the state when it happened."

"Hey, Darcy!" she yelled, causing Netty and me to jump. "Bring me a drink!" She turned and smiled. "This is turning out to be a nice day. I get my things back, and my enemies are being taken down. Of course, I already knew about Rob, but it's good to know Linda might be next."

I had to try hard not to look disgusted. Sally wasn't a very forgiving or sympathetic person. Still, I didn't think she was behind any of it. Darcy, on the other hand…Could she be doing these things to get revenge for her mother? If she was, I didn't think Sally knew. While I was blaming everyone, I might as well add Netty. I should probably tell the sheriff that if I was found dead, he should question her. She was still giving me nasty looks. I wanted to stick out my tongue, but that wouldn't do anything for my image.

"I wonder who killed Rob," I said. "Do you have any guesses?"

Sally rubbed her chin. "Hmm. My guess would be Linda's stuck-up daughter. I've heard she hated him. She probably wouldn't hurt her mom, though. Linda spoils that girl like nothing I've ever seen. It's gonna kill her someday when she has to go out and get an actual job. She thinks hanging around the diner with her phone is work."

Darcy came in and handed her mom a large cup. Sally grabbed it and quickly drained it. Darcy pursed her lips and looked disapprovingly at her mother, but she didn't say anything. My guess was that Darcy was the one keeping things afloat over here. She was probably the reason the house looked so neat, just like she was the reason Rob's house looked nice.

"Well, I guess I should go. If the rest of your stuff turns up, I'll let you know."

"Thanks for bringing this to me," Sally said, holding up the brooch. "It was the most important."

I stood and nodded. Darcy followed me to Rob's car, and Netty followed. Darcy absentmindedly ran a hand over her braid and chewed on her lip. She would probably be really pretty if she didn't look so stressed.

"Thanks for letting me in," I said, unlocking the car.

She nodded. "I know you probably think my mother is involved, but she wasn't. She can hardly get around any-more."

I shook my head. "I don't think she was." There was no reason to add that I thought Darcy might be. Darcy nodded and went into the house. Netty stayed outside, her arms crossed, looking at me like I was diseased.

I turned to the side, covered my mouth, and let out three belly coughs. They were so exaggerated they hurt my chest. Netty's brows jumped from her head, and she covered her mouth and ran into the house, slamming the door behind her. I might have smiled.

Chapter 13

"Did you know Darcy Peterson was cleaning for Rob?" I asked José when I got back to the diner.

José started the dishwasher, and his mouth turned down. "No. That's strange. I'm surprised Sally would allow that."

"I wonder if they are having money problems. Sally didn't disguise the fact that she hated Rob and Linda."

"I've never known Sally to keep a job for longer than a month. Darcy has always done a bunch of odd jobs to keep them afloat. I'm surprised they even let you in the house."

I grabbed a rag and ran it under the hot water. "Darcy didn't want to let me in. Her daughter, Netty, definitely didn't like me. I think she might be scared of germs. She looked at me like I was the most disgusting person on the planet."

José laughed. "That sounds like the queen. She let you know she was named after a queen, right?"

I smiled and wiped down the counter. "She did."

"I feel bad for the girl. She doesn't like anyone. Every time I see her, she's sneering at someone or telling her mom that people aren't behaving the way they should. I think she's spent most of her life cooped up with Sally while Darcy works."

My smile slid away. I probably shouldn't have teased her. "Where is her dad?"

"He disappeared about five years ago. He seemed like a decent guy, but a good guy doesn't walk out on his family."

"That's sad."

"Yep. I think Darcy would have done alright if it hadn't happened. They seemed happy together, but she had to move back in with Sally after he left. Sally was lucky that she had inherited her house from her parents. Without it, they would have a lot more trouble than they already do."

"I think I'm going to stay at Rob's house for a while. Just to see if I find anything. Now that I know Darcy worked for Rob, I think I can look at things differently."

José's eyes focused on me. "You don't suspect Darcy, do you?"

I shrugged. "I don't know. She looked guilty when I brought up the stolen things, and then she left the room."

The door burst open, and Boyd entered. His plaid shirt was untucked as usual, and his face was a little red. "Did you all hear?"

"Hear what?" I asked, tossing my rag in the sink.

"You know Toby Richards?"

"No."

"He was one of the names on the sticky notes from yesterday. Rob stole some stuff from him. Today, Toby found them on his porch."

I tilted my head and tapped on my chin. That changed some of my ideas. Why would someone steal the things Rob stole and then return them to their rightful owners?

José put a pan of rolls in the oven. "Maybe the thief isn't the murderer. Maybe they were trying to fix something Rob did."

"But who would want to do that?" I wondered.

"Maybe just a Good Samaritan."

I shook my head. "No way. They blew up my car."

"Right. It's something to think about, though. I wonder if any of the other things were returned. We still have a long day of cooking ahead of us, so we can't check until later."

"I can," Boyd said. "I'll ask around and see what I can find out."

"It still doesn't make sense. There is no way anyone would know we were digging that stuff up. We didn't even know until right before we did it."

The bell above the door rang, and a group of ten people entered. There wouldn't be time to think for a while. The diner steadily got more and more people in every day as word got out about José's food and my desserts. We should probably capitalize on it before Linda found out.

José put out a few trays for Livy and Sarah, and I went into the lobby to see if anyone wanted a cookie. It almost seemed silly to ask because almost everyone did, but it was good to get to know the customers.

Barbra, Opal, and two other women sat at one table, laughing about something. When I stopped at their table, they all smiled at me.

"Would you ladies be interested in a cookie today?" I asked.

Barbra grinned. "You better believe it. I don't even have to feel guilty because I'll be at Zumba tomorrow to work it off!"

Opal groaned. "I'm still sore from the last time. I'm too old to start new things. My waistline doesn't need a cookie, but I'll take one just the same."

Barbra patted her arm. "If you take care of yourself, you might be around a lot longer."

"I suppose. I'll take two cookies."

The door opened, and Jett entered. I wondered if he had any clothes besides his sheriff's stuff. If he did, I had yet to see it. He glanced around until his eyes fell on me, and then he pointed at the kitchen. I excused myself and followed him in.

"Hey, Sheriff Jett," José said, piling a plate with food. "What's new?"

"Two people have had the things Rob stole from them returned."

I nodded. "We knew that one person had."

"Which one?"

José set the plate out for Livy. "Toby."

Jett took out a pad of paper and scribbled something on it. "I didn't know about Toby. I wonder if everything was returned."

"Boyd is out trying to find out," I said.

Jett's mouth turned down. "You all really need to tell me things before you go off investigating on your own. It is my job."

I handed him a double chocolate chip cookie. "But you don't have any help. You might as well let us do some of it. Are you ever off duty?"

His shoulders slumped. "Not really. I mean, I technically am, I guess, but there's no one else to go to around here."

I smiled as he shoved the entire cookie in his mouth. "I was wondering if you owned any real people clothes."

He grinned. "Real people clothes?" he said, covering his stuffed mouth. He chewed for a minute and swallowed. "I might own a pair or two."

José laughed. "I saw you running in shorts and a T-shirt one time and almost didn't recognize you."

"I admit, it's pretty sad. But what am I going to do?"

"Deputize Boyd?" I suggested. That made everyone laugh.

"If he were trained, I would. He's a bit old to be running after criminals, though."

"Muddy Creek is pretty small. Is there really that much crime?"

"Not a ton, but enough to make it difficult for one person. We've had more than our fair share of drugs and domestic disputes."

"I'm surprised about the drugs," I said. "The population seems a little old for that."

José loaded up another plate. "Are you saying old people can't do drugs?"

"No, I just always think of that as a younger thing."

Jett snatched another cookie from the cooling rack. "Most of the drug problems have been with the younger population. By younger, I mean about forty. Most of the teenagers in the town have managed to avoid drugs, as far as I can see."

"Have you ever had trouble with Darcy Peterson?" I asked.

He shook his head. "Nope. Sally, yes, but not Darcy."

José grinned. "What about Netty? We were just talking about what a ray of sunshine she is."

Jett laughed. "Netty likes me. She comes in about once a week and brings a list of people she wants me to arrest."

I pulled a pack of butter from the fridge. With Jett around, I might need to make more cookies. "I might be on her list this week."

Jett leaned back against the counter. "Oh?" He shoved the cookie in his mouth. I really needed to make them bigger, so he couldn't do that.

"I actually feel a little guilty," I admitted. "She was furious when I sneezed near her, and I might have coughed just to annoy her."

Jett pulled a pink piece of folded paper from his pocket and opened it. He raised his brow and read, "Pretty woman with blond hair and mean eyes came into my house and got germs everywhere." He smiled at me. "She even added three exclamation marks."

"Wow. She's fast. I thought she was the one with the mean eyes."

"At least you admitted to it. That saves me the trouble of hunting down the pretty blond woman. I can just arrest you here."

I turned toward the mixer, hoping he wouldn't see my face turn pink. "Ha, ha. You better be nice, or I won't make you any more cookies."

"You're making them for me? I'm flattered."

I put the butter in the bowl and shook my head. "You are impossible."

He chuckled. "I'm going to go check with some other people and see if their items were returned. Maybe I'll find Boyd and let him join me."

Turning, I watched him grab a few more cookies and smiled. "See you around."

He waved and left the diner.

José laughed quietly, and I realized I was still staring at the door, smiling. I turned and glared at him. "What?"

"You like the sheriff."

I narrowed my eyes. "Of course I do. I like all of you."

He grinned. "You know what I mean."

For the second time in two minutes, I felt my cheeks heat. "I do not."

"Whatever you say."

"I don't."

He shrugged, still smiling. "Okay."

"Stop it."

"Stop what?"

I crumpled up the butter wrapper and threw it at him. It was a foot short and fell harmlessly to the floor.

He laughed. "You're only making yourself look more guilty."

"Don't you have anything to do?"

He handed a plate through the window to Sarah. "Yep, and I'm doing it."

I went into the pantry to grab some sugar and let my face cool down.

"It's nothing to be embarrassed about. The sheriff is a good-looking man. I think you should go for it."

I crossed my arms. My face must be glowing. I was going to have to stay in the pantry a little longer. "I didn't come here to find a man."

"Sometimes life throws you a pleasant surprise. He isn't seeing anyone, you know."

"I don't care," I lied. I had wondered, but I didn't want to ask anyone.

"He hasn't dated anyone in years."

"He's probably too busy."

"Maybe. I'm sure he would find time for the right person."

I rolled my eyes. "That's nice." I grabbed the sugar and took it to the mixer. "What about you? Are you dating anyone?" Two could play this game.

"Nah, I'm too old for that."

"Nonsense."

"It's true. I'm set in my ways. Besides, if I found someone, how would I know they weren't just using me for my mad breakfast-making skills?"

I laughed. "You can make a pretty good breakfast."

Chapter 14

I climbed into a nice, fluffy bed in the guest room at Rob's house. I had used my phone as a flashlight to find where I was going because the electricity had been turned off. The bills weren't in my name. I wondered what I would need to do to change that. Technically, I owned the house until I decided what to do with all of Rob's things. I hadn't brought Creepers's bed because he would sleep on my face anyway.

The sheets were stiff, and I wondered if anyone had ever slept here. Probably not. It didn't sound like Rob was very social. The bed was cozy, and I thought about taking it to the diner. The mattress I had purchased did the job but was far from comfortable. Moving it might be hard. It was too big for Rob's car. I thought about Jett's truck but wouldn't ask him to use his work vehicle to help me.

I fell asleep quickly and woke up somewhere around midnight. My eyes were wide as I stared into the darkness in front of me. Someone was moving around downstairs in the house. I sat up and tried to decide what to do. I didn't want to panic if there was no reason. It could be Jett, looking for clues.

I grabbed my phone from the nightstand and squinted as the bright display penetrated my tired eyes. I turned down the brightness and went to my contacts, scrolling down to Jett's name. He answered on the third ring.

"Hello?" His voice was groggy.

"This is Ivy," I whispered. "I'm at Rob's house, and I think someone is sneaking around."

"Did you see anyone?"

"No. I'm upstairs, and I can hear something downstairs. Probably in the kitchen. The electricity is off, and I don't have a flashlight."

"Get in a closet and stay there until I come. Call José and have him stay on the line with you."

The phone clicked, and I quickly called José. There was no answer. Creepers looked up at me from his spot on a fluffy pillow, but he wasn't interested in anything I was doing. I got out of bed and walked carefully across the plush carpet. It wouldn't be good if I alerted the intruder to my presence. Whoever it was probably thought the house was empty. My blown-up car came to mind, and I decided I wouldn't stay in the closet. What if they burned down the house to destroy any evidence?

The darkness was like nothing I'd experienced. My hand seemed invisible in front of my face. I inched across the room, holding my hands out in front of me. I reached the door and slowly made my way to the stairs. I grabbed the railing and stood at the top, hoping Jett would be fast. It felt like I was waiting forever. I could hear someone going through things in the kitchen. If they were looking for something, they would be disappointed. We had already searched everything.

There was nothing to see up here, so I slowly descended the stairs. When I was about halfway, I sat down and tried to look through the wooden railing. The kitchen was behind the stairs, so all I could see was a faint light bouncing around. My heart felt like it was going to burst from me.

Footsteps were coming away from the kitchen. I held my breath and watched the light move closer. The person passed the stairs, walking right by me. They were heading for the front door. If I didn't do something, they would get away. Where was Jett? I tried to make out who they might be, but they must be wearing black. Why hadn't I paid the electric bill?

I stood slowly and walked down the next few steps. When they passed by the base of the steps, I jumped. I didn't know what I was thinking. I aimed for the dark shadow and gritted my teeth as the two of us fell to the ground. A woman screamed, and I did my best to hold her down. She struggled to get up, but fear helped me keep her down. I felt my fingers catch on her hair, and she yelled out. Her hair was too long to be Tania.

The front door burst open, and Jett stood there holding a lantern and a gun. I looked down to see Darcy Peterson. I jumped to my feet and ran over to Jett.

"Darcy?" he said as we watched the woman get to her feet. She dramatically brushed off her black pants and glared at me.

"Why did you attack me?" she demanded.

I narrowed my eyes. "I own this house. You're trespassing."

Darcy folded her arms, and her lip trembled. "I didn't mean any harm."

"What are you doing here?" Jett asked. "This isn't looking good for you. Go sit in the kitchen."

Darcy sighed, and we followed her into the kitchen. Jett held up his lantern, and we all sat around the table. Jett put the light on the table and leaned toward Darcy. "Explain."

"I didn't kill Rob," she said.

Jett rested his elbows on the table and steepled his fingers. "No one said you did." Eerie shadows bounced across everyone's faces.

"But I know that's what you're thinking."

"How about we worry about Rob later? What are you doing here now?"

She slunk down in her seat. "I was just looking to see if any of my things were here."

"Why would they be?" he asked.

She shrugged. There were a few items on the table. I was pretty sure they hadn't been there the last time I was here. There was an unopened package of white candles, a bracelet, and a book. They were all things that we had dug up from under the willow.

"I can't be sure Rob didn't steal anything from me."

"You were his housekeeper. He wasn't at your house," Jett said.

"That's not the only reason she was here," I said, pointing at the things on the table. Darcy looked at the table and frowned.

"What's the other reason?"

"These things are some items we dug up. The things that got stolen. She was returning them because they weren't labeled with sticky notes. She stole them from the backyard."

She sighed. "Yes, I did. I had hoped that I could find my mother's things. I didn't have time to look through it all, so I grabbed all the boxes. I felt bad, so I returned everything to its rightful owners. These were the only things that I didn't know what to do with, so I brought them back. I wasn't stealing because everything was already stolen. I didn't mess with Linda's car or kill Rob. Everything would get cleaned out eventually, so I wanted to make sure I got Mother's brooch and other things."

"You blew up my car!" I accused. "I understand wanting your mom's things back, but that was going too far."

"I didn't blow up your car!"

I raised my eyebrow. "It just blew up on its own?"

She pressed her forehead against the table. "I can't go to prison. Netty needs me."

I opened my mouth to speak, but Jett shook his head. I hadn't meant to take over his job.

"Darcy?" he said. "If you didn't blow up the car, what led you to the backyard?"

She looked up. "I came to the house because I wanted to look for the brooch. The lock doesn't always latch right in the back, and I thought I might be able to get in. I was inside when you all came. The garage seemed like a good place to wait until you left. After a while, I heard you all talking outside. I looked out the window and saw you all digging. When the car exploded and you all ran, I hurried over to see what you had been doing."

My eyes narrowed. "So you took everything?"

"I didn't know what the explosion was, and I didn't know how long you would be gone. I figured all the boxes there were the things I was looking for. I didn't have time to search through them, so I just grabbed everything and ran."

"But you didn't find the brooch and the necklace because I had put them in my pocket."

She nodded. "There were some other things that belonged to my mom. I separated it all out. I was going to wait a while to give it to my mom. At least until I found the brooch and necklace."

Jett leaned forward. "I understand why you did what you did, but that doesn't make it right. You interfered with a case, and now I'll have to investigate you. You might say you didn't blow up the car or kill Rob, but this looks bad."

Darcy bit her lip and nodded.

"You should have talked to me and let me know about the brooch, and you shouldn't have returned things to the other people. It could have all been evidence."

"I'm sorry," Darcy mumbled.

"Right now, I want you to go home. Don't come into this house or onto the property again. Do you understand?"

Darcy nodded and stood.

"Stay in town."

She nodded again and hurried from the room. We heard the door slam as she left the house.

"I don't think she killed Rob," I said.

"Me either. I'm still not sure about the car, though." He ran his hands through his hair and yawned. "What are you doing here at this time?"

"Sleeping."

"You moved in?"

I rubbed my lips together. "No…I just thought I might figure something out if I stayed here for a while."

"Look, Ivy. This isn't your case. It's not up to you to put yourself in danger."

The shadows from the flickering lantern bounced across his face, making him look more serious than he probably was.

"I know, but someone is trying to make me look guilty. I can't just sit around and hope they don't succeed."

"You don't need to worry. I'm going to figure it out. It's my job, and I'm trained to do it. You aren't."

I frowned. "Maybe not, but I've seen almost every old crime show episode. And I read every Nancy Drew book ever written back in junior high."

He chuckled. "That hardly qualifies you."

"I also watch *CSI* and *Psych*. Does that help?"

He smiled. "No, not really."

"Come on. I totally took Darcy down so she couldn't get away before you came. I'm going to have a bruise on my knee to prove it."

His smile disappeared. "That was a stupid thing to do. You could have hurt yourself. Don't do anything like that again."

"If I hadn't, we wouldn't have known who it was."

"Yes, but what if you had gotten hurt? Or worse. I want you to stay away from here for now."

"You already told me I probably shouldn't stay above the diner. I can't stay away from everywhere."

"At least in the diner, you have other people in town. Out here, you are more vulnerable."

I wanted to argue, but he was right. I could still remember the fear running through me when I woke up and heard Darcy. That was an experience I didn't want to have again.

"Get dressed, and I'll follow you into town and make sure you get to the diner in one piece."

Heat crawled over my neck. I hadn't realized I was in my pajamas. My very silly pajamas covered in donuts with faces. My mom always gave me funny pajamas for Christmas. I always acted appalled, but they were always really comfortable. They were my go-to when they were clean. I jumped up and ran up to get dressed and grab Creepers, but I slowed down on the dark stairs. I didn't want to trip and embarrass myself even more.

Chapter 15

I slept in the following morning. When I'd gotten back to my bed at the diner, it had been after two in the morning, and I'd had trouble falling asleep. Creepers pawing at my head didn't help. The smell of bacon made my stomach growl. I took a quick shower and pulled my hair into a neat braid. I threw on some mascara and went to the kitchen to help José and Larry.

"Good morning," José said, flipping an egg. "Bad night?"

"Kinda. Where's Larry?"

"Sick."

"He sure misses a lot."

"Yeah. I'm pretty sure Linda only keeps him on because no one else wants to work here. You want some breakfast?"

He handed me a plate of eggs and bacon. I sat on a stool and grabbed a fork.

"Thanks."

"Jett was in here a half hour ago. He told me what happened last night. You need to be more careful. Sorry I didn't answer your call. My phone was off."

"It's okay. It all worked out."

"Jett said he told you to stop helping."

I speared a piece of egg. "He told me."

"But you aren't going to listen."

"What makes you think that?"

"Because I had a thought."

"Oh?"

"The bolt cutters had a price tag on them. The only place around here to buy tools is at Hal's. He has cameras everywhere."

I took a bite and thought for a minute. "Did you tell Jett?"

"Yeah, I told him yesterday, but he's probably too busy to look into it."

"Do you think Hal will let us watch the videos?"

"Wouldn't hurt to ask."

"We don't know when the bolt cutters were purchased. It could take forever to watch that much camera footage."

José's mouth turned down. "I guess you're right."

"We could go watch some of it. I mean, it's possible they were only purchased a day or two before. Or maybe Hal keeps records of who buys what."

"It's worth a try. You wanna go after work?"

"Sure."

José put more eggs on a plate. "There probably aren't many pairs of bolt cutters purchased around here. I wonder if we could narrow it down by asking Hal when he last sold any."

"Good idea."

The back door opened, and Tania came in. "Smells good."

"You were gone for a while," I said.

She shrugged. "I wanted to make the most of it."

"Did you meet the guy?" José asked.

"Oh, yeah. He was pretty lame. People on dating apps always are."

I decided she wouldn't appreciate me pointing out that she was on the dating app.

"So what did you do?" I asked, cutting my bacon.

"Oh, this and that. I was not made for small-town life. I love being able to go shopping and pick a movie. Our theater is so pathetic. They could at least have two choices."

"Who took care of your mom while you were gone?" I asked. I hadn't even thought about it before.

"No one. She can get around fine with her crutches. She said you never even checked in on her."

"I've been busy and didn't know you would be gone for more than a day."

"My mom isn't happy with you."

"Why? For not checking on her?"

"No. She heard you were getting José to cook all sorts of different stuff."

"From who?"

"I might have let it slip."

"Did you also let it slip that the diner is making a lot more money?"

She pursed her lips. "Hmm. No, I didn't think about that. Can I talk to you for a minute? Outside?"

I shrugged and put my plate down. Now my eggs were going to get cold. I followed Tania out back and shut the door.

"What is it?"

She put a hand on my shoulder. "Ivy, you know I always have your back, right?"

"Okay?"

"I've been talking to my mom, and we think you are probably the one who killed Rob."

I stepped away from her. "What?"

"It just makes sense. Why would someone plant that stuff on you? Anyone would assume you weren't here when Mom's accident happened. We think you drove down here, cut her brake line, and left before anyone ever saw you. I really thought I saw you at the store that one day."

"If you thought you saw me, wouldn't you have come up to see what I was doing in town?"

"I didn't have time."

"What would my motive be?"

"Getting the diner."

"That's unreal."

"Hey, I'm just saying what it looks like to everyone."

"To everyone, or to you? Who have you been talking to?"

"I haven't talked to anyone but my mom since I returned." She shot me an insincere smile. "Let me help you. I can help you get out of town."

"No. I didn't do it, and I think you know it. Why would I want the diner? I've spent almost no time here."

"Yeah, well, your mom said you recently lost your job. Desperation can drive people to do crazy things."

"This is unreal."

"The entire thing is. I am worried, though. If you get rid of my mom and Rob, I'm next."

I crossed my arms. "Why would you be next?"

"Next on your way to getting the diner."

I moved my jaw from side to side. Tania didn't know that I would inherit the diner before she would. I wasn't sure if that was something I should share with her. If she really was the murderer, that would put me in danger. None of it added up.

"I'm not having this conversation with you," I said, turning.

"Why don't you go home? That won't look like you're running."

"She can't," Jett said, coming around the side of the diner. "No one on my list of suspects can leave town."

Tania's eyes sparkled even though she frowned. "So she is on your list?"

"Yes, but only because I need to prove it wasn't her. I have to do a thorough investigation."

Tania gave me a slight smile. "It must be awful to be a suspect in a murder."

"You're also on the list," Jett said. I wasn't positive, but I think he enjoyed saying it.

Her eyes went wide. "Me? Why?"

"Just because you're on the list doesn't mean I think you did it. Like I said, I just need to cross off anyone who could be involved from my list. You shouldn't have left town. I thought I was going to have to go find you."

"There is no way it could have been me."

Jett shrugged. "You had access to your mom's car and your uncle."

"But I wasn't here when Ivy's car blew up."

Linda didn't know about my unfortunate car experience. Jett told me to keep it from her for now. I opened my mouth to tell Tania this, but Jett discreetly shook his head. Tania hadn't been here when the car blew up, so how did she know?

"Just stay in town."

Tania's frown changed into a smile. "Sure thing. I was planning something fun. If you're going to keep me here, I hope you intend to keep me company."

I raised my eyebrow, but Jett's expression remained blank. Tania waved over her shoulder and walked over to her Jeep. She got in and drove off.

We stood and watched her as she disappeared around the diner.

"I keep telling her she can't drive back here," he said.

"How much did you hear before you came around the corner?"

"Most of it. When I got to the diner, José told me you were out here, so I hurried around."

"I don't get it. I don't know if she did it or not, but she has to know it wasn't me."

"She's trying to scare you and get you to run. If you run, you look guilty."

"Should I go talk to Linda?"

"I wouldn't. She'll probably tell you more of the same stuff that Tania did. If Tania confessed to it all, I don't think Linda would fault her. She refuses to see anything but her perfect child in Tania."

"She's always been that way. Even when I was young, I noticed, but Tania and I were closer back then, so I didn't care. Where is Linda's car?"

"It's about forty miles away in a tow yard."

"What made you check the brake line?"

Jett shifted and looked thoughtful. "It all seemed like an accident. I probably wouldn't have checked anything, but Tania told me she thought she had seen someone by the car the night before."

"Tania seems to see a lot."

"She does, doesn't she?"

Chapter 16

José and I sat in a small back room of the hardware store. A desk sat in the corner and several screens on the wall showed different places in the store. Way more than I would think a little business would need. When we walked through to get to the back, I counted six aisles, and they were small.

"What can I help you with?" Hal asked. He was a tall, husky man with thick dark hair and a goatee. He rocked back and forth on his computer chair.

I cleared my throat nervously. I didn't want to seem snoopy. "We are wondering if you keep track of all the tools you sell?"

"Of course. We have it all on file. We've had a lot of theft over the past five years, so we keep close track of everything."

That explained the cameras. "Would you be able to tell us the last time someone bought a pair of bolt cutters?"

He leaned back in his chair and rested his elbows on the armrests. "Ah, I see. I've heard you two have been sniffing around with the sheriff. Did you get your wires crossed? Sheriff Malone already came in and asked me the same thing not two hours ago. The last time the store sold bolt cutters was the day of Linda's crash at five thirty-five."

I leaned forward. "If you have the exact time, then you should be able to pull up the surveillance, right?"

"Sure. The sheriff already watched it."

José tapped his fingers against his knee. "Did he say anything?"

"He asked me to save five minutes of the video following the woman who bought the bolt cutters and send it to him in an email, then he left."

"Can we see it?" I asked.

"I don't see why not. I have it saved right here." He turned the computer at his desk to face us. "I need to go up front. Just push that button and watch it as many times as you want." He got up and left the room.

José reached forward and pushed play. It wasn't the best quality. The video showed a woman in a black hoodie and jeans enter the store. She kept her head down so we couldn't see her face. Her head was covered by the hood, and she had long blond hair coming out of both sides.

My mouth turned down, and I felt sick. "That looks like me."

José nodded. "Sure does."

The woman walked slowly down the first two aisles and grabbed what must be the bolt cutters. She walked to the front, paid, and then left. José started it again. It was hard to watch.

"She planned to set you up from the beginning," José said.

"Who?"

"Tania. It has to be her. Besides your hair, you look a lot alike. If she threw on a wig, it wouldn't be hard for her to be mistaken for you."

"I wonder what Sheriff Malone is thinking."

"He's a smart guy. He won't be fooled."

I sighed as José sent the video to his email. "I don't know why you trust me so much. You've known Tania a lot longer."

"You bet I have. And I've never trusted her. You're different, and people can see it. Tania is in for herself."

"I would think it was me if I didn't know it wasn't."

"Don't stress about it. Maybe you should go search your aunt's house. Tania might have left some clues."

"That won't be easy. Linda hasn't been leaving the house." I felt defeated. There was no way Jett wasn't going to think it was me.

"Linda likes things to be the same all the time. She always left the diner to take a siesta around two. You know Tania isn't hanging around at home, so maybe you can sneak in tomorrow and check it out."

"But if I get caught, I'm not sure what I would say. You heard Tania. Linda thinks I'm the guilty one."

"We can get Boyd to stand as the lookout. Linda can't get around very fast, so Tania is the only one we need to worry about finding you. If she isn't home, it should be fine. If Tania comes home, Boyd can distract her. Two is a slow time. I might go with you if Larry shows up."

"Do we tell Jett?"

He rubbed his chin. "I don't think so. He would probably tell us not to get involved." We stood and walked through the store and out into the warm air.

"Where does Tania go all the time? There isn't a lot to do around here."

"She spends a lot of time at the pool, and I think she goes to other towns quite often."

I kicked at a rock. "I'm going back to my room. I think I need more sleep, and I have a Zumba class tomorrow."

"Alright. I'll see you tomorrow."

"Good night."

"Good night. And remember, you don't need to worry. We are going to figure it all out."

I nodded and walked down the sidewalk toward the diner. José went the other way. The sun was still up, but

I didn't care. I hadn't slept well since coming here, and it was all catching up with me. I unlocked the diner and climbed up the steps to my room. Creepers walked lazily over to me and rubbed against my ankles. After I locked the door, I checked on the cat's water and filled the food bowl. I yawned and kicked off my shoes, then collapsed onto my mattress.

The fact that I was innocent wasn't helping me feel better. The woman in that video...it had to be Tania. I rolled over and stared at the wall so the sun wouldn't shine in my face. Having a west-facing window wasn't convenient right now. I was a little surprised Jett hadn't come over to arrest me. I would have if I were him. Maybe he needed more evidence.

I closed my eyes and tried to turn off my mind, but it spun a million miles an hour. Strangely enough, that was the last thing I remember thinking. I don't even remember dreaming or Creepers crawling onto me. I woke up at six in the morning. I jumped up, pulled on my exercise clothing, and ran to the studio for Zumba.

My students were all waiting outside for me. "Sorry, I'm late!" I said, unlocking the door.

"It's alright," Barbra said, stretching her leg. "We were all just catching up."

Opal caught the door when it opened. "I don't mind. If you're late, that's less time for me to be in pain."

"You really don't have to do it," I said. "It's all voluntary. I can refund your money if you would like."

"No, no. I like to complain, but it's been fun. I've even had a bit more energy."

"If we come to class, we get to hear all the gossip," Barbra added.

My heart thumped. "Gossip?"

Barbra punched me playfully on the arm. "Hal said you came into his store to see the evidence against you. He said his surveillance showed as clear as day that the person who tried to kill Linda was you."

My face flushed. "There was nothing clear about that tape."

"Don't worry, sweetheart. None of us think you did it."

"Of course we don't," Boyd said.

I rushed in and turned on the music. I started dancing and noticed that we were missing a few people. Those were either the people who thought I was guilty or the ones who made a goal to get fit and then gave up. I saw it all the time. I'd been there more than once. Exercising was a commitment that was always hard to start and stick with.

The door opened, and I glanced to the side, half expecting to see Sheriff Jett Malone with his handcuffs ready for me. It was Tania. She was wearing the same pink workout clothing that Barbra liked to wear.

"Hey, all!" she called over the music. "I thought I would join you today."

"That's thirty-five bucks," Boyd said, walking over and holding out his hand. I wasn't sure when Boyd had become my unpaid employee, but he seemed to enjoy it.

Tania sneered. "You are actually charging people for this?" She shook her head but pulled out her wallet. I kept moving and watching my class. It had taken me time to get used to teaching without calling out the moves. Zumba was funny that way. I'd taught aerobics before Zumba, and it was a lot different.

My smile widened as Tania joined the group, and she spotted Barbra. Tania's mouth turned down, and Barbra grinned. "Twinners!"

Tania rolled her eyes, then pulled a water bottle from her bag and took a long drink. I was feeling a little self-conscious. She might be wearing the same outfit as a seventy-year-old woman, but she wore it well. I was sure Tania would have something to say about my baggy T-shirt the next time we talked.

The door opened again, and this time it was the sheriff. I felt my stomach drop. He stood in the doorway with his arms crossed.

"What's happening, Sheriff?" Barbra asked.

That was when I realized I'd stopped moving. My entire class was looking at Jett.

"I bet he's here to arrest Ivy," Opal whispered loudly.

"Well, we aren't going to let that fly, are we, girls?" Barbra said. She stepped in front of me and crossed her arms. "If you want to take Ivy, you have to get through me."

If I hadn't been horrified, I would have laughed. Barbra was at least four inches shorter than me, and, well, seventy. A few of the others came and stood next to her. It was sweet the way they believed in me—or at least didn't want me going to prison.

Boyd stood in front of all the women. "We aren't letting you take her, Jett. She's lifted the morale around here with her baking and all."

Jett pressed his lips together, and his eyes sparkled. If I didn't know any better, I would think he was trying to hide a smile.

Tania stepped closer to Jett. "Ladies, as much as I hate to say it, if Ivy has broken the law, then we need to let Jett arrest her. No one is more broken up than me."

I turned off the music, and my shoulders slumped. It wasn't like any of this was a surprise.

Jett raised one eyebrow. "Why does everyone think I've come here to arrest Ivy?"

"Isn't that why you're here?" Barbra asked.

"No. I was looking for Tania, and someone said she came in here."

Tania grinned. "You wanted to talk to me?"

He opened the door, and she followed him. I felt like crumpling to the floor and crying with relief, but who knew what would happen later? I could still end up in jail.

Barbra patted my arm. "Come on, honey. Let's get back to dancing."

"Wait! Look outside," Opal said, pointing at the glass door. "I think the sheriff is arresting Tania!"

Every head spun toward the scene on the sidewalk. Jett was holding a pair of handcuffs, and Tania had her hands on her hips. I could hear her voice but couldn't make out what she was saying. Jett took a step toward her, and she punched him in the nose and ran. Jett covered his nose and took off after her.

"Oh, my!" Barbra said. She pushed open the door and yelled, "You get her, Sheriff!"

The entire class filed out the door to see what was happening. I could hear everyone cheering Jett on. I grabbed my purse. There was no way I was going to get everyone back on task, so I might as well go to the diner. News of what happened would eventually reach me there.

Chapter 17

"I don't think we need to search Linda's house anymore," I told José later that day. Everyone who came into the diner was talking about Tania getting arrested. We had more customers than I'd ever seen, and I didn't think I would be able to slip away to go to Linda's anyway.

"Why not?" he asked, flipping a hamburger. "We have to strike now. I doubt Jett will be able to keep Tania for long without a lot of evidence...although I think punching a lawman is an arrestable offense."

"We don't even know what he arrested her for. All we know is what everyone is speculating. She could have a bunch of unpaid parking tickets or something for all we know."

I picked up my phone and glanced at it. "I can't believe Linda hasn't called me. Do you think she even knows Tania was arrested?"

"News travels fast."

"But Linda's house is out of the way."

"Someone always wants to be the bearer of bad news. I bet someone told her. If they didn't, we have more reasons to go today."

I shook my head. "I don't want to be the one to tell her."

"We can let Boyd do it. That will distract her while we search."

"Even if Tania is responsible for Rob's death, I doubt she has evidence lying around her room. She would have to know that someone might search."

"Unless she thought she had blamed you so well, there wouldn't be any other suspects."

I scratched my ankle. The chiggers were out in full force, and the little critters liked to bite my legs. "Even if we want to, the diner is really busy. I don't think we can slip away."

"Larry will be here at noon. Everyone coming in to catch the gossip will be long gone before two, and things will be quiet."

"Alright." I wasn't feeling up to it, but I needed to make sure I cleared my name. If I wasn't a coward, I would ask Jett why he arrested Tania. I'm not sure whether he would be able to tell me, and it was driving me mad. I was dying to know what he thought about the video surveillance from Hal's, but that would be an awkward thing to ask about.

Today, I was making snickerdoodles. They weren't as good as my chocolate chip cookies, but they were almost as addicting. I might tease the sheriff and Boyd about eating too many cookies, but the truth was, I could eat five cookies before I even started to feel like it was too much. If I had a glass of milk, I could eat even more.

As I mixed the dough, my mind kept going back to Tania. I was almost positive she was the one from the video. I kept telling myself over and over like it was a new revelation. The why part still eluded me. If it had only been Uncle Rob's death, it would make sense. But Linda's crash...I couldn't imagine she was behind that. I still didn't know if Tania even knew she had been third in line to get the diner.

I suddenly stood straight and turned off the mixer. I turned to José. "What if there were two different crimes? What if Tania killed Rob but didn't mess with Linda's car?" I sighed. That didn't even make sense. "Never mind. Tania bought the bolt cutters. That would tie her to Linda's car, not Rob."

José looked thoughtful. "What if Tania bought the bolt cutters, but she didn't use them? It's possible that whoever did it stole them from her garage."

"That doesn't explain the long blond hair. Why would she need to disguise herself if she was innocent? Who puts on a wig to go to the hardware store?"

"Right." He placed the burgers on plates. "You might be right about it being two crimes, though. It felt like they went together because they were in the same family, but they could be completely unrelated."

I grabbed the cinnamon and measured a few teaspoons into a small bowl. "I thought I was figuring something out, but the crimes have to be related. Whoever is trying to blame me planted things related to both crimes."

José sighed. "That's right."

"This is so frustrating. I always thought trying to solve crimes would feel more exciting and less like a headache."

"It's gotta be worse when someone is trying to blame you."

"That's probably it." We stopped talking when Larry came in. He barely acknowledged us as he put on his apron and pulled on a hairnet.

The next couple of hours slowed, just like José predicted. We left Larry in charge and picked up Boyd on our way to Linda's house.

Boyd sat in the back and drummed his fingers on the back seat. "So I go in and ask Linda if she knows Tania is in the clinker?"

I nodded and turned onto a dirt road. "If she doesn't know, I'm sure she'll get really upset. If she does, she'll probably want to vent to someone about how unfair it all is. Either way, just keep her talking."

"Got it."

"And if she seems suspicious—"

"Oh, she won't," Boyd said. "Linda's used to me babbling about everything."

We stopped before we got to the house, and I pulled the car back behind some trees off the side of the road. They weren't really covering the car, but no one would see it unless they were looking. We got out of the car and walked through the trees and weeds, avoiding the road. I bet the chiggers were feasting on my ankles. There had to be a way to keep the little buggers from biting.

"There's the house," José said. "Ivy and I will go in from the back. You go first, Boyd, so she won't hear us."

"Alright." Boyd bent at his waist and ran from tree to tree, hiding.

José chuckled. "Why is he hiding? It's not supposed to be a secret he's here."

I smiled. Boyd was a fun character. Once he got out of the cover of the trees, he stood tall, walked confidently up to the house, and pounded on the door. A moment later, he opened the door and let himself in. Linda must have called out to him.

"Ready?" José asked, pulling a pair of gloves from his pockets.

"Yep," I said, putting on my own. We snuck around to the back of the house and tried the door. It was unlocked. We crept into the small mudroom and paused to listen. I could hear Boyd talking, but I didn't understand what he was saying.

We stepped over piles of laundry, trying not to make a noise on the tile floor. I slowly pushed open the door, cringing when it squeaked. I froze for a moment but kept going when I heard Linda talking normally. She must not have heard.

I led José up a carpeted staircase. Every step made a creaking sound that I hoped couldn't be heard throughout the house. When we got to the top, we made our way to Tania's room. It wasn't locked, so we went in.

"Linda and Boyd are in the living room," I whispered. "We aren't over it, so we should be okay if we keep it quiet."

José nodded and got down on his hands and knees to look under the bed. I went to the accordion doors on the closet and pushed them open. Tania wasn't messy like Linda. Her room was decorated in light pink. The curtains were pink, which made the beige walls appear pink. Her queen-sized bed had a dusty-rose comforter and pillow.

I couldn't see anything suspicious in the closet. Her clothes were all neat, and her shoes were all placed in rows on a shoe rack. I reached up to feel the shelf, but nothing was up there.

"I don't see anything," José said. "I don't want to look in her drawers."

"I will." I walked over to her chest of drawers and opened the top one. It was full of socks. I pushed them around, then moved to the next drawer. Nothing but underwear. The next one had folded jeans. I picked up a few pairs and gasped. There was something that looked like hair.

"What is it?" José asked.

I reached in and pulled out a long blond wig.

José grinned. "Busted."

"Maybe. Tania likes to dress up. Just because she has a wig doesn't mean she used it to impersonate me."

"But she probably did. Who wads up a wig and shoves it in a drawer? Let's keep looking."

I put the wig back in the same place I found it. I didn't want Tania to know we had been here. We spent another ten minutes searching but didn't come up with anything else, so we snuck back out.

When we got to the car, I slapped my forehead. "We forgot to figure out a way to let Boyd know we were done. We can't just leave him here. It's a long walk back to town."

"You could go to the door and ask Linda a question about the diner."

"She's probably pretty upset about Tania. She might think I'm being insensitive."

José shrugged. "Do you have another plan?"

"No," I admitted.

"I'll wait here."

I groaned and walked back to the house. I knocked on the door and heard Linda yell something. I assumed she said for me to come in, so I let myself in. I entered the living room to see Linda in her favorite spot. It was the only place I'd seen her since I came.

"I can't believe you're showing your face here." Linda glared at me.

I flinched. "Why?"

"Because of you, Tania is in jail!"

"I don't see how it's her fault," Boyd said.

Linda's mouth puckered. "Because she is the one who is behind it all! She wants the diner."

"I've never wanted the diner. As soon as all of this is tied up, I'm leaving."

"I don't want you in the diner anymore. I can't have a murderer running my business."

My teeth scrape together, and I tried to relax my jaw. "I'm not supposed to leave town. I need to stay in the room at the diner or I won't have anywhere else to go. You should know I'm innocent."

"Tania is innocent. Jett will figure it out soon enough."

"I'm going back to town. Do you need a ride, Boyd?"

He stood. "That would be appreciated."

We left with Linda calling something after us. I didn't catch most of it, but I got the gist.

José had pulled the car over closer to the house. He must have assumed it was okay since Linda knew I was here.

"Did you find anything?" Boyd asked, climbing into the back seat.

José moved back to the passenger seat, and I got behind the wheel. "We found a wig."

"That sounds promising."

I turned on the car and backed up. "We should probably tell Jett about it. Then he would know where it is if he gets a search warrant."

José shook his head. "If we tell Jett we were snooping around Tania's room, it might make it sound like we planted evidence."

"Linda is really mad at the sheriff right now," said Boyd. "She was telling me about how her lawyer is going to get Tania out and put Jett in prison for slandering her good name. She had a lot to say about you, but it doesn't need repeating."

"I could have guessed that." I tried to act like I wasn't bothered, but I was. Linda wasn't ever what I would call a doting aunt, but this trip had cemented my resentment. She had to know it wasn't me. I'd come a long way to help her, and she didn't seem to appreciate it at all. I should be spending my time looking for an actual job, not investigating a murder, but I had to make sure things turned out right.

Chapter 18

Whipped cream was a hard thing to make pretty. Especially if you didn't use the stuff that sprayed out of a can. I liked the spray can as much as everyone, but when it came down to it, I liked the taste of the whipped cream that came in the big container better. It didn't dissolve as easily as the spray stuff. Someday, I'd try homemade, but not when I was in a hurry. I plopped a big blob onto a piece of shortcake and placed a bunch of strawberries on top. It wasn't the prettiest dessert I'd ever made, but it would taste fabulous.

"It's looking good," José said. "You better speed up, though. The dinner crowd hit early today." He grabbed the plate and put it out for one of the servers to take.

I grabbed a bunch of plates and started slapping blobs of cream on the cake as fast as I could. Looks didn't matter.

That was what I kept telling myself. Larry swayed to his music as he peeled potatoes in one corner, and José was grilling up steaks. Anyone who ate at Linda's this evening would go home well-fed.

I looked at my work and felt almost satisfied. With luck, everyone would want dessert today because there was a lot. After washing my hands, I started placing the cake on the window shelf for Sarah, Kate, and Livy.

"Do you guys need help?" I asked José. There was no point in addressing Larry. He wouldn't hear me over his music.

"It looks like Jett is done with his steak," José said without turning. "Why don't you take him some strawberry shortcake?"

"Are the servers busy?" I asked. I hadn't even known Jett was here and wasn't sure I wanted to talk to him. Why was it all even happening? I didn't know why I felt guilty about things I didn't even do. It'd been a curse my entire life.

"Not too bad. You're going to have to face him eventually, or you'll look guilty."

I frowned and grabbed the dessert. He was right. I walked into the lobby and pasted a smile on my face. No reason to feel guilty. I didn't do it.

"Hey, Ivy," Jett said as I approached him. "I sure hope that cake is for me."

My smile became more sincere. "It is." I placed it in front of him.

He grabbed his fork and took a big bite. He closed his eyes and sighed. "That is sooo good. You should open a bakery."

I beamed. "Thanks. I'm glad you like it." I turned to walk away, but he grabbed my wrist.

"Hey, can you sit for a minute?"

My heart started racing. "Sure." I sat on the bench across from him. "What's up?"

He looked around and leaned over the table. "I had to let Tania go," he said so only I could hear. "I'm sure she's guilty, but I don't have enough evidence to keep her. She's really mad. I just wanted to warn you."

I swallowed. "Warn me?"

"She knows I'm on to her, and she's obviously trying to get you involved. Stay away from her if you can. Do you think you can leave the diner for a while?"

"Right now?"

"Yes."

"Let me go talk to José." I hopped up and hurried to the kitchen. When I got there, Larry was gone, and José was trying to watch the steaks and potatoes at the same time.

He glanced at me. "Hey, Ivy. Can you flip those steaks?"

I rushed over and grabbed a spatula. "Where's Larry?"

"Tania must have escaped or something. She stuck her head in the back door and yelled for Larry to come out, and he dropped everything and left. They must be standing by the door because I heard her yelling at him a minute ago."

"What was she saying?"

"I couldn't make it out."

"Jett said he had to let Tania go because he didn't have enough evidence."

José sighed. "He needs to go search her room."

"Jett wants to talk to me, but I can't leave you short-handed."

"Go, I'll manage."

The door opened, and Larry stomped in, slamming the door behind him. He walked over to the potatoes and started peeling again, muttering something to himself.

"Go," José mouthed to me.

I went back out to find Jett. He was stuffing the last bite of cake into his mouth. When he saw me, he got up and threw some bills on the table. We walked outside, and Jett opened the passenger door to his truck. He motioned for me to enter. I pulled myself up into the truck and buckled my seat belt. I didn't know if we were going somewhere, or if he just wanted to talk where no one would hear.

He climbed into the driver's seat and put one hand on the wheel. He turned to me. "I shouldn't admit this, but I don't know what to do about Tania."

I cocked my head and watched him. "Oh?"

"The worst thing about working in a small town is that I know everyone. I grew up with some of them. Arresting people I know is so awkward."

"I bet."

"Tania punched me in the nose."

I gave him a sympathetic smile. "So I hear."

"I had to wrestle her down and throw her into my truck while the Zumba class all cheered me on."

"At least they were cheering for you and not against you."

"I guess. It's really annoying I couldn't keep Tania locked up."

"Even though she hit you?"

He shrugged. "I didn't charge her with that."

"Why?"

He shrugged again.

"Embarrassed to get hit by someone you dated?"

His mouth turned down. "I didn't date her."

I smiled. "Right."

"I feel like I'm missing something. I watched the surveillance from Hal's, and it's obviously Tania."

"You think so? When I watched it, I was sure it was me even though I knew it wasn't."

"You watched the video? How?"

"Hal showed it to us."

His eyebrow rose. "Who is us?"

"Me and José."

"I thought I told you to let me handle it."

I shrugged. "We just watched the video."

"I need to have a talk with Hal. He shouldn't be showing that to anyone but me."

"What do you think is missing?"

He ran a hand through his hair. "If I knew, it wouldn't be missing. I think I'm not understanding a rational motive for Tania. She's close with Linda. If it was just Rob, it would make more sense."

"What made you think it was Tania and not me in the video?"

"For one, you weren't in town. Someone would have seen a strange car, and no one did. Then there were Tania's bands."

"What bands? The ones she dips in lavender to keep the bugs away?"

"Yes. Her socks were over her pants, and the bands were on top of her socks. She does that when the chiggers are bad."

"How did I miss the bands?"

"You probably weren't looking for them. I watched it over and over before I thought to look for them."

"Isn't that evidence?"

"Yes, but even though Tania bought the bolt cutters, that doesn't mean she used them. Anyone tampering with the car could have gotten them from the garage."

"Did you ask her about it?"

"She admitted to buying them but said they were stolen."

I tapped my lip. "Hmm. What is Tania's relationship with Larry?"

"They dated for about a year. I think they broke up last month. Why?"

"When I went back into the kitchen to talk to José just now, Tania was out back yelling at him."

Jett narrowed his eyes and stared blankly at the diner. "Interesting. From what I heard, she dumped him."

"I'm surprised he kept working at her mom's diner."

"He needs a job. There aren't a lot of them around here."

I started to get excited. "What if they only broke up to throw you off? What if he's in on it all? I can't really imagine Tania getting down on the dirty ground to tamper with a car. She probably doesn't even know what a brake line is."

Jett gave me a half smile and turned the key.

"Where are we going?"

He started backing up. "To take Larry's garbage."

"That sounds exciting. Do I get to help you sort it?"

"Sure thing."

We began driving slowly across the square. "There is something else."

He chuckled. "Do I want to know?"

"Probably not. I snuck into Linda's house and searched Tania's room." I left José and Boyd out of it.

He groaned. "And?"

"I found a blond wig in her drawer."

"Is that all?"

"Yeah."

"That won't be very helpful since she admitted to buying the bolt cutters."

"But it shows she was trying to disguise herself."

"That's true. Larry lives right up there," he said, pointing.

"Anything important is probably gone. He probably threw anything worth looking at away when it happened."

"Have you noticed how much garbage is piled up behind the diner? The garbage is only taken every two weeks."

"Oh good," I said sarcastically. "We can sift through two weeks' worth of garbage."

He grinned. "And lucky for us, today is garbage day, so he won't be suspicious when it disappears."

Chapter 19

Larry's garbage covered the entire sheriff's office. It smelled like a mixture of garlic and dead animals. I didn't envy whoever had to clean it when we were finished. The office had a small front room with a desk and a computer. Behind it was a hallway and two holding cells. We had dumped most of the trash in the hallway but opened one of the cells when we needed to spread it out.

Jett was looking over some papers he found. "So what would Nancy Drew do?" he asked.

I kicked at a container, trying to see inside. "Well, she would probably walk into one of the cells, and someone would capture her, tell her their plan, and then she would escape."

"So she doesn't figure anything out until someone tells her?"

"She figures stuff out. She gets captured a lot, though. It's been a long time since I've read them. They were my middle school reading obsession, and that was a long time ago."

"Nothing exciting here," he said. "What would Jessica Fletcher do?"

I laughed. "I don't know. It's been too long."

"I thought you were the queen of boring mystery shows."

I eyed him. "They aren't boring."

He just smiled and kept flipping through the papers.

Larry must eat a lot of tuna. I was glad we were wearing gloves because I didn't want to get his gross stuff all over me. "How does one person have this much garbage? Two weeks shouldn't add up to this much." He obviously ate lots of prepackaged meals and had at least ten empty milk gallons.

"He shares a bin with the neighbor next to him. Some people do that to save money."

I bent down and picked up a large towel with a yellowish-brown stain. "What do you think about this?"

He looked over and dropped the papers. "That could be something. What does it smell like?"

I smelled it and gagged. "Fish."

He walked over and took the towel, giving it a smell. "I bet it's brake fluid."

"Yes! We got him!"

"Maybe. I need to have someone who actually knows what they're looking for look at it. I'll take it to the city in the morning."

"Should we go through all the other stuff? Just in case?"

"Probably. We don't want to miss anything."

"Do you think I can look at the place where Linda crashed?"

"I don't see why not. It's just a broken tree. I looked all around and didn't see anything suspicious. You can see where the car went off the road because it had rained the day before, and the tracks going down the hill are still there since it hasn't rained again. It just seemed like an accident until I saw that clipped brake line."

"Was it on a dirt road?"

"Nope. It was paved."

"Hmm. Were there any skid marks?"

"No. I think with the brakes out, she just went right off the road with no resistance."

"Will you take me there when we're done here?"

"Sure."

Chapter 20

J ett pulled his truck over to the side of the road, and I got out. We were on top of a medium-sized hill. The wind was blowing, making the temperature bearable.

"Her car went off over here," Jett said, pointing at tire marks in the dirt.

I frowned. The tire marks were perpendicular to the road. "She must have made a really hard turn to go off like that."

Jett's brows came together. "I didn't think about that."

"If her brakes didn't work, it seems like the car would have gone off at more of an angle."

"Maybe she panicked and overcompensated."

"I guess that's possible." I took off down the hill, walking next to the tracks. I let myself go faster than I should have, and I wondered if I would end up flat on my face. Jett was probably following me, but I didn't want to look over my shoulder and lose my balance. I could see the broken black walnut tree. The car must have hit the side because that was the only place with damage. I got to the bottom and ran a few feet past the tree as I tried to stop.

Jett chuckled behind me. "Nice run."

"Ha, ha." I walked around the tree but didn't know what I was looking for. It was a tree that was hit by a car. There was nothing strange about it. I crossed my arms and puckered my lips, moving them to the side.

"I told you. Nothing exciting."

I looked at the undamaged trees nearby. "How far did you search?"

"Only around the tree."

I scanned the ground. The tire tracks went right to the tree. There were a few pieces of plastic, probably from the bumper.

"When did the car get towed?"

Jett rubbed his chin. "I think it was the next day."

"So the ground was already hard? I don't see any tracks from the tow truck."

"Yeah, it was boiling the next day. If you look closely, you can see faint lines where the truck drove up." He pointed at the ground, and I squatted down to see. The tracks were really light, especially compared to the car tracks.

Jett glanced around. "The tow truck didn't come down from the top. It came from the side."

I stood and walked in a big circle around the tree. When I didn't see anything, I went wider. I stopped when I came to a small stream. A little trickle of dirty water, only about six inches wide and maybe three inches deep, ran by.

"You found the creek," Jett said.

I wrinkled my nose. "That's a creek? It's small."

"That is Muddy Creek."

I laughed. "This is what the town is named for? That's pretty sad."

"It's not always like this. It fluctuates quite a bit. East of here, it gets pretty deep."

"Uncle Rob wanted his ashes thrown in here. They'll just sink to the bottom."

"Probably."

"Hey down there!" someone called. I jumped and looked at the top of the hill. Boyd and José stood there, waving.

Jett waved back. "It looks like your posse is here."

"We're coming up!" I yelled back.

Jett rubbed his ear. "Warn a person when you want to scream like that."

I just smiled and started up the hill.

"The diner is closed already?" I asked when we reached the top.

"Already?" José asked. "It's past nine o'clock."

"It stays light so long here."

Boyd looked down the hill. "Is this where Linda crashed?"

Jett nodded. "How did you find us?"

Boyd shrugged. "Barbra said she saw the sheriff's truck coming this way. We just drove until we saw it."

"Did you find anything?" José asked.

I shook my head and glanced up at Jett. "Any chance we can go see Linda's car?"

"Nope. The tow company is closed tonight, and I have too many things to do."

"So you want me to take you home, Ivy?" José asked.

Jett pulled out his keys. "I can take her."

I wanted to go with Jett, but I could probably get José to take me to the tow yard.

"I'll go with José," I said. "Then we can talk about tomorrow's menu."

We said goodbye to Jett, then the three of us got into José's car.

"Are we going to the tow yard?" Boyd asked from the back seat.

"Of course we're going to the tow yard," José said, starting the car. I smiled. I didn't even have to talk anyone into it. José knew where to go, so I settled back for the drive.

"Maybe you should quit the diner and become Jett's deputy," I teased José.

He laughed. "I don't think so. This is fun and all, but I'm too old to do more than snoop. Cooking is my passion, and I think I would miss it."

"Do you know how much security the tow yard has?" I asked.

"I doubt there's much, but that's only a guess. What is anyone really going to steal? It's just a bunch of trashed cars."

"Car parts are a pretty hot item," Boyd said. "I bet they have a lot of security."

"What if we get there, and we can't get in?" I wondered.

"Then we camp out until morning."

"But José and I need to be at the diner."

"You could leave me there and come get me tomorrow night. I don't mind wandering around the city."

It was dark now, and there wasn't a lot of traffic out. I leaned my head against the window and tried to work through my thoughts. A huge yawn felt like it might break my jaw, and I closed my eyes. I must have fallen asleep because the next thing I knew, the car stopped.

"Here we are," José said, killing the engine.

I rubbed my eyes and looked at the dark shop in front of us. The building was small, and the sign was off. One tall light in the parking lot made it possible to see where we were. We got out of the car, and I looked around for any blinking lights that might be cameras. I didn't see any. We walked over to a ten-foot chain-link fence that started at the side of the building and went around back. I pulled out my phone and flipped on the flashlight.

"It's like a car graveyard," Boyd said. "That fence is too tall for me."

I hoped we could find the car. I wasn't completely sure I remembered what it looked like. "You two can stay and keep watch." I put my foot in one of the small openings and started climbing.

"I'm coming," José said. I felt the fence near me shake when he started climbing.

I got to the top and threw my leg over and started going down. It felt like I was making more noise than normal, but it was probably just because it was so quiet outside. I jumped to the ground and waited for José.

I shined my light around, but all the cars looked the same to me. "Why are there so many cars here? Don't they end up at the junkyard?" I whispered.

José pulled out his own phone and turned on the light. "They aren't all junk. Cars get towed for lots of reasons. Some can get fixed; some are repossessed. Cars get towed if they are parked illegally."

"Do you see Linda's?"

He walked around, shining his light, and I followed. "Here it is." I walked around the dark car and studied the damage. Most of it was on the driver's side. I could tell where it had hit the tree. It was no wonder Linda's leg was broken. I peeked into the window and tried to make sense of what I was seeing. The steering wheel was crushed against the front seat, and the airbag limply surrounded it.

The back seat looked untouched. I wished it was lighter. Everything was covered in shadows. Food wrappers and empty gas station cups littered the floor. Linda didn't keep her car any cleaner than her house.

I heard a sound off to the side, and I froze. José rushed over to me, his finger up to his lips. He bent down, and I followed. I pushed myself against the car and tried to quiet my breathing. I was breathing a lot harder than I should be, considering I had only been peeking into windows for the last five minutes.

I gritted my teeth and closed my eyes. Should we stay, or make a run for it? I couldn't decide. Running wouldn't work well since there was a tall fence we would have to get over. There was a low growl, and my eyes popped open. A large doberman stood in front of me, his ears pointed straight up and his teeth bared. I stood slowly, and so did José.

José grabbed my arm and crept toward the front of the car. Any second, the dog was going to pounce on me, and that would be the end.

"Get on the hood," José said quietly.

I jumped on the hood and climbed to the roof. José was right behind me. The dog kept growling but didn't jump at us.

"Now what?" I asked.

"No idea," José said. "Maybe he'll get bored and leave."

"I doubt it. He's probably trained for this type of thing. I bet he just keeps us here until morning, and then we'll get arrested."

"I'll text Boyd."

I looked over at where Boyd should be. It was too dark to make him out. "Boyd can text?"

"Well, he's not the best at it, but he can read them. Sending one back isn't so easy for him."

I waited while José messed with his phone. I thought about calling Jett, but for all I knew, he would have us arrested. I didn't really think he would, but it was possible. That would be a last option. Even if he came for us, it would take a long time for him to drive here, and he wouldn't be happy. He'd already told us he had a lot to do.

A shrill whistle came from Boyd's direction. The dog shifted his head and took off toward the fence. José and I both flew from the car and ran in the opposite direction. We climbed the back fence, and I practically fell over the other side. I hit my knee on the sidewalk, but I didn't stop to see if it was bleeding. We ran around to the front. The dog was barking at the fence now, and it wouldn't be long before someone noticed we were here.

Boyd saw us, and the three of us all jumped in the car and sped away. I buckled my seat belt with shaky hands. I couldn't believe the dog hadn't gotten us. He must not be fully trained because he got distracted way too easily.

I relaxed against the leather seat. "That was the most terrifying moment of my entire life."

José laughed. "It reminded me of being young. I wasn't always the best-behaved teenager."

"Did you find the car?" Boyd asked.

"Yes, but it was too dark to see very much," I said. "It was probably a waste of time." My face felt funny, so I put a hand to it. It was wet. "I think my cheek is bleeding."

José handed me a tissue, and I held it to my face.

"Did the dog get you?" Boyd asked.

"No. I wonder if it happened when we went over the fence. I was so scared I probably wouldn't have felt anything."

"That's adrenaline for you," Boyd said. "You should see how fast I used to move when I was doorbell-ditching flowers—"

I turned and looked at his dark shape. "Flowers? For who?"

He scratched his head. "It doesn't really matter. It was a long time ago."

I wouldn't pry tonight. I was too tired, and I owed Boyd for distracting the dog. Without him, the evening might have gone a lot differently.

Chapter 21

"That looks awful," José said the next day. He was scrambling eggs while the ham sizzled on a skillet.

I pursed my lips and touched the cut running down my cheek. The thin cut hurt more than it should have. I'd tried to cover it with makeup, but that had been a disaster. I'd ended up washing it off, and that had stung.

"I know. Everyone in my Zumba class was asking about it this morning."

"What did you tell them?"

"That I was climbing a fence to get away from a dog."

"Did they ask any more questions?"

"No. Once the subject of dogs came up, I lost them all. They spent the rest of the time talking about dogs they've known over their lives. It was hard to get anyone dancing."

There was a knock on the front door. We didn't open for five more minutes. I walked over and saw Jett through the glass. I sighed and unlocked the door. He stepped in, and I angled my face so he wouldn't see the cut.

"Morning," he said.

"Morning. Have a seat, and I'll have something right out." I hurried toward the kitchen.

"Wait," he said, stopping me in my tracks.

"Yeah?" I said without turning.

"You didn't, by chance, go to the tow yard last night, did you?"

Guilt settled in my stomach like a rock. "Why would you think that?"

"Oh man. You did, didn't you? I called the tow company this morning to see if I could come check the car out again, and they said someone jumped the fence and made their dogs go crazy last night."

"Dogs? There was more than one?"

"What were you thinking?"

I still didn't turn. "I just wanted to see the car."

"You're lucky the dogs didn't attack you! You could also get arrested for trespassing. José? I know you can hear me. Did you take Ivy to the tow yard?"

José peeked out the kitchen window. "Yes. Sorry, Jett."

He sighed. "I bet Boyd was with you, too. You guys can't do this. It's not your job, and it's dangerous. You could have been hurt."

Now I really didn't want to let him see my face. "It was fine."

"Why won't you look at me?"

I threw my hands in the air. "Why would you want me to look at you?"

"Ivy?"

"What?" I knew I was being obnoxious, but I was sure my face was red. That, with the cut, was not what I wanted Jett to see.

"She cut her face on the fence," José said.

"Thanks a lot, José," I muttered.

I could hear Jett stomping toward me. He grabbed my arm and turned me to face him. "Ouch. That's going to leave a scar. This is what I'm talking about. You shouldn't be doing things like that. No more, okay? Be patient and leave it to me."

"That's easy for you to say," I said, crossing my arms. "I need to clear myself."

"You aren't even on my list anymore, and I never thought you were guilty, anyway. I had some people from the city do some checks, and it shows that you were using the internet from your apartment on the day the bolt cutters were purchased and the day before and after the crash."

Relief flooded through my body. "Why didn't you tell me that before?"

"I only got the confirmation last night."

"That doesn't clear me from Rob's death. His death might not have been connected to Linda's crash."

"I think they are."

"Maybe."

The door to the diner opened, and a couple came in and sat at a booth. I hurried to the window shelf and grabbed two steaming plates, and took them to the people. I went back for another and placed it on the table for Jett.

When I returned to the kitchen, I saw Larry putting his apron over his head. I stopped and stared at him, then quickly glanced away. All talk of the murder had to end, especially since he was a suspect now.

Livy rushed in, her ponytail bouncing behind her. "Sorry I'm late!"

"Only by a minute," I said. "Don't worry about it."

She grabbed a purple apron and hurried out to greet people. The servers' aprons were a lot cuter than the white ones we wore in the back. I was trying to come up with a fun dessert for today, but my mind kept going back to Linda's car. Something about it was bugging me.

"What?" Larry asked, pulling one earbud from his ear.

That was when I realized I was staring at him. "Sorry, just zoned out."

He nodded and went back to his music. I really wondered why Linda didn't try harder to get someone more reliable than Larry. There had to be someone out there that needed work. I thought about Darcy Peterson. She was obviously okay with working for someone her family didn't like. I wondered if she could cook. I couldn't imagine Sally cooking and someone at that house had to do it. They hadn't ever been to the diner so they must eat at home.

"What's wrong, Ivy?" José asked.

"I don't know what to make."

"Make your chocolate chip cookies."

"I've already made them more than once."

"So? Everyone loves them. They are the most popular things I've ever seen here."

I nodded and went for a mixing bowl. I'd made the recipe so many times that I could do it without thinking. I grabbed the butter and peeled off the wrapper. When I went to throw it away, the garbage was full. We must have missed it yesterday. Linda really should hire someone to clean and not expect the cooks and servers to do it. I pulled out the bag and tied the ends into a knot. It was heavy, but nothing I couldn't handle. I hauled it out the back door and over to the large dumpster. I threw it into the empty bin and cringed at the smell.

When I turned around, I almost bumped into Larry. I'd never realized how tall he was before. I took a step back. "Hey."

His eyes narrowed, and he put one hand against the garbage bin near my shoulder, blocking me in on one side.

I wondered if I should scream. José and Jett would probably come running.

I smiled. "I'm going to make cookies." I felt ridiculous, but I didn't know what else to say.

"I'm sure you are. Little Miss Perfect, coming to change everything."

"You don't like change?"

"Not when it comes from someone like you. I know what you're trying to do."

I blinked. Larry had never said more than three words at a time to me. I wished he would go back to doing that. "I don't know what you mean."

"You want to take Tania's diner."

"The diner is Linda's, and I have no intention of doing that. I'm only staying until Linda is better."

"Stay out of things."

I gulped but looked into his eyes. "What things? Murder?"

Larry blinked. "Murder? What are you talking about?"

The door opened, and Jett stepped out. "What's going on out here?"

Larry walked to the door, pushing his shoulder into Jett as he went in. "Absolutely nothing."

Jett walked over to me, and I tried to stop trembling. One of these days, I was going to get control of my emotions.

"Are you alright? What did he say?"

"It was nothing," I said, trying to brush it off.

"You're shaking."

"I'm fine."

"Ivy, what did he say?"

I told him quickly, and his jaw tightened. "We need to wrap all of this up, and we need to do it soon. The longer it takes, the more dangerous things could become."

"When are you taking the towel we found to get it tested?" I asked, trying to forget about Larry.

"I took it early this morning. They said they will call me later today."

"So if it's positive, you can arrest Larry?"

He sighed. "Having a towel covered in brake fluid doesn't make a person guilty, but I will talk to him."

"I don't want to spend the day cooking around him. Has he ever had trouble with the law before?"

"He's been arrested a couple of times for substance abuse."

"Opioids?"

"No, and I want you to stay out of it. I've got it, alright?"

"I need to start the cookies," I said, turning and walking back to the diner.

"Ivy," he said sternly. "Promise you will let me handle it."

I smiled over my shoulder. I was still nervous about Larry, but I wasn't giving up. Jett looked at the sky and shook his head, then followed me. When I entered the diner, I heard my phone chime. I pulled it out of my purse and frowned.

"What is it?" Jett asked quietly at my side.

"My mom is here. She's at Linda's right now."

"Good."

"How is it good?"

"I called her and told her she should come."

"You what?" I said, a little too loud. Larry and José both looked at me.

He raised his eyebrow. "Shhh. You need someone on your side."

"Once she knows what's going on, she's going to freak out!" I whispered loudly.

"I explained it all to her yesterday."

"Now she wants to have a family dinner tonight and talk about everything. You better not have put my mom in danger."

"I'll come."

"To the family dinner? It will probably be a family fight, and I'm sure Tania and Linda don't want to see you."

Jett grabbed my elbow and led me back out to the porch. "It'll be fine. I'm not scared of Tania and Linda, and your mom sounds like a reasonable person."

"She is, but that doesn't mean she should be here."

"She understands that family relationships can be complicated and has your back. She knows you are innocent, and she's upset about your aunt accusing you the way she is."

I put my hand to my cheek. I'd been hoping I wouldn't see my mom until the cut looked a lot better. She was going to worry.

Chapter 22

I stood outside Linda's house and watched my mom walk toward me. "Mom, you shouldn't have come," I said, giving her a hug. "I can deal with this."

"Linda is my sister, and I should be here when she isn't at her best. I know she hasn't treated you well. I should have been the one to come help. What happened to your face?"

I shrugged. "I climbed a fence and scraped it on the top."

"It looks painful."

"It's fine. I can't believe Jett called you."

"Jett? Sheriff Malone?"

I'm sure my face turned pink at the least. "Yes."

My mom pushed back her light brown curls and smiled. "I'm guessing Sheriff Malone isn't an old man with missing teeth."

I rolled my eyes. "Almost everyone calls him Jett, and he's invited himself to dinner."

"Lovely. I tried to talk Linda into having a small funeral for Rob, but she is insistent on following his wishes. It seems strange not to celebrate his life at all. There's no closure."

"Did Linda tell you she thinks I'm behind all of it?"

She patted me on the shoulder. "That's just Linda. She's always quick to accuse. I think she just wants to protect Tania."

"I think Tania is behind it."

Her mouth turned down. "Really?"

"She's trying to frame me. It's making me really mad. Her and her ex. I think it was her plan, but he pulled it off."

"That's terrible, but I don't find it hard to believe."

The front door opened, and Tania poked her head out. "Are we going to eat?"

"The food is in the car," I said, turning and opening the hatch. I'd volunteered to bring food from the diner so Tania couldn't poison us all or anything. Tania disappeared back into the house without offering to help carry anything. Jett's truck pulled up, and he climbed out. He was wearing jeans and a red T-shirt. It was the first time I'd ever seen him dressed down, and he looked amazing.

"Hmm. Not bad at all," Mom said. I realized I was staring and went back to pulling things from the car.

"Need help?" Jett asked, walking up.

"Sure." I handed him a big container full of enchiladas. My mom grabbed the rolls, and I got the salad.

"I'm Jett Malone," he told my mom.

"Candy Clark. Nice to meet you. Thanks for calling me."

"Sure thing."

We filed into the house and brought everything to the kitchen. Tania was sitting at the table texting someone, and Linda was sitting at the head with her leg propped up.

"Who cooked the food?" Linda asked as we placed it on the table.

I glanced at her. "José."

"Oh good. Should I call him to confirm it?"

My brows came together. "José and Larry cook the food. I only do dessert."

Linda put on the most pathetic face I'd ever seen and looked at my mom. "Candy, you can't believe the trouble this girl of yours is causing at my diner. She's changing the way I do things and ruining the ambiance I've worked so hard to establish."

I tossed some napkins on the table. "You told me to figure it out, and I have. José said we are taking in four times the diner's usual amount."

Linda's eyes shot daggers at me. "It's not all about money."

I wanted to ask what it was about, but my mom shook her head, so I bit my lip.

"If the diner wasn't bad enough, I'm almost sure she caused my crash and killed Rob."

My mom sat down and grabbed a roll. "Oh, Linda. You know that isn't true. Ivy was in her apartment sick on the day of your accident."

"Maybe. When we talked, you told me she had been sick, but that you weren't in contact during that time. She could have come here and cut my brake line, then hurried back home."

"Nope. We have confirmation that she was home at the time," Jett said.

Linda looked disappointed.

"I don't know why you want to pin everything on me," I said, sitting next to my mom. Jett took the chair across from me next to Tania. Tania glared at him and scooted farther from him, looking back at her phone.

"Everything is falling apart," Linda muttered. "Sheriff Malone here even had the audacity to arrest Tania the other day." Tania's face turned red, but she didn't look up from her phone.

Jett leaned back and crossed his arms. "And I'm pretty sure I'm going to do it again once I get the evidence."

Tania looked up and frowned. "I did not mess with my mom's car, and I didn't kill Rob! All I did was buy the stupid bolt cutters!"

The room went silent, and Linda started fanning her hand in front of her face.

"Why did you buy the bolt cutters?" Jett asked.

"Because we didn't have any."

I wrinkled my nose. "You just got up one day and thought, gee, I don't have any bolt cutters, so I better go get some?"

She shrugged.

Jett raised his brow. "Why did you wear a wig and try to frame Ivy?"

She slammed her phone onto the table. "I wasn't trying to frame her. It's just a coincidence the wig looked like her hair. I swear it's the truth. This is all stressing me out! That's why I ran off to Wichita. I needed time to think, and I didn't want to take my phone and have anyone track me."

It was just like Tania to try to turn herself into the victim.

I heard the front door open and slam shut, and Larry came barreling into the kitchen. He turned to Tania, his eyes burning.

"Get out of here," Tania hissed.

He pointed at her and glared. "I'm not going down with you, Tania." She jumped to her feet and tried to push him from the room, but he wasn't budging. He turned to Jett. "I cut the brake line for Tania."

Linda's brows came together, and she put her hands to her cheeks. "Tania?"

I sucked in a breath as it hit me. "He cut it after the accident."

Larry nodded. "I didn't hurt anyone."

Jett frowned. "That doesn't make sense. Why?"

I slapped the table with my hand. It was all coming together. "Because there wasn't an accident."

Linda's eyes narrowed, and she pointed at her leg. "I beg to differ."

"I saw the car. The steering wheel was smashed into the seat. Your leg is the only thing that was hurt. If you had been in the seat, you would have been pinned down and a lot more hurt than you are."

"Ridiculous!" Linda growled. "You see how she's slandering me, Candy?" My mom just stared.

"You weren't in the car," I said. "You pushed it down the hill. That's why the tire tracks were perpendicular to the road. If your brakes had gone out, you wouldn't have gone off the road the way you did. It would have been more gradual."

Jett leaned forward. "And your car went off at the top of a hill. If the brakes weren't working and you weren't pushing on the gas, the car wouldn't have gotten all the way up to begin with."

Larry nodded. "Tania called me and said she needed a favor. She asked me to cut the brake line. I thought she might give me another chance if I did it, so I ran to the crashed car and cut it. I figured it wasn't hurting anything."

Jett stood. "Why confess now?"

Larry shrugged. "I'm not in the gossip circles in town. I keep to myself. Cutting brake lines is one thing, but I just heard that people think whoever did that killed old Rob. I don't want any part of that, so I came clean."

Everyone looked from Linda to Tania.

Tania covered her face. "I didn't kill Rob!"

"Why have the brake line cut?" Jett asked.

She sighed. "I saw my mom hurrying toward the house that day. She doesn't like to run, so I figured something was wrong. When I opened the door, she started crying and limping and said that she crashed into a tree. We called for an ambulance. I knew she was lying because I'd seen her running, and she hadn't freaked out until she saw me."

"This is absurd," Linda muttered.

Tania glanced at her mom, then down at her hands. "Mom wanted a new car, but we couldn't afford it. I figured she did it for the insurance money. After the ambulance came, I ran and got the bolt cutters and had Larry mess up the car. I wanted it to look like it wasn't Mom's fault so we would get the insurance money."

"What about my car?" I asked.

Larry dropped his head. "I did that as well. I'll admit to what I've done and go to jail, but not for murder."

"What does my car have to do with anything?"

Tania wiped away a tear. "I couldn't remember if I'd worn gloves when I put the bolt cutters in your car. I didn't want Jett to find any evidence."

I pressed my lips together and tried to keep my anger in check. "I understand you wanting to help your mom, but you tried to pin it on me! How is that okay? I could have gone to prison."

Tania picked at her long fake nail. "Better you than my mom. And I still tell you, I didn't kill Rob."

"But you tried to frame me, and the medicine bottle was also planted on me. Why would multiple people try to frame me?" I stared up at the popcorn ceiling and tried to think. What were we missing? "You must have planned it in advance since you told your mom you thought you saw me the day of the accident."

"No, I didn't. The wig was really a coincidence, and then my mom randomly asked me if I thought I saw someone who looked like you in town. She asked me three times, so I finally said yes, since I knew that's what she wanted me to say."

"Linda?" Jett said. "Do you have anything to say?"

"I'm not saying anything without a lawyer."

"Who was the doctor that wrapped your leg?"

"I'm not saying."

"I will find out eventually. Why make it harder?"

My eyes fell to the top of the fridge. Linda's canister with chocolates was gone. My heart sped up, and my eyes widened. "The crash wasn't for insurance."

Jett's brows knit together. "What do you mean?"

"The crash was to make it harder to prove Linda killed Rob."

Chapter 23

"**I** did not kill Rob!" Linda bellowed.

"Where are your chocolates?"

Linda's eyes jumped from the fridge to me. "What are you talking about?"

"The chocolates you keep on the fridge. You said Rob always sneaks them. Where is the canister?"

"It broke."

"I think you made the chocolates and filled them with opioids. You knew Rob would steal them eventually, and he is always drinking, so there was a good chance it would kill him."

"I don't know why I invited you here. You've been ungrateful the entire time, and now this."

"I think you invited me so you had someone to work for you for free and then someone to eventually pin the murder on."

"Why would I kill Rob? And why would I frame you? None of this makes sense."

"It might," Jett said. "Everyone in town knows you've always spoiled Tania. She's thirty years old, and you still bend to her every whim. You didn't want the diner to go to anyone but Tania. You got Rob out of the way, but that would still leave Ivy, and you didn't want to kill her, but you were still alright with having her put away for murder. That way Tania gets the diner, no questions asked."

Tania shook her head. "That doesn't add up. I would get the diner after Mom dies, not Rob."

Jett turned to her. "Actually, you wouldn't. Your grandma's will was a little strange. She made weird conditions. The diner would go to Rob at her death, and then to Ivy. You were after Ivy."

Tania's teeth ground together. "Why? It should go to me. I'm the one who has worked here all these years."

"I wouldn't have taken it," I said. "Linda worried for nothing."

"I can't believe this, Linda," my mom said. "How could you?"

Linda stood and glared at everyone in turn. "I did not kill Rob! He killed himself! I put my opioids in one chocolate and placed it in *my* canister on *my* fridge. He chose to steal it. If he had been honest, he never would have died. I have no blame in any of this."

Larry shook his head. "Even I can see the holes in that logic."

"If you placed the opioids in the chocolate with the hope of someone eating it, then you are guilty of murder," Jett said.

Linda's face turned red, and she pointed at me. "I will not allow her to have my diner! It should go directly to Tania, and I will stop anyone who gets in the way!"

Jett walked toward her, and she took a few steps back. She walked on her foot without a limp. "Run, Tania!" she yelled.

Jett turned to Tania. "Stay where—"

"Ahhhhhhh!" Linda yelled, charging Jett. He wasn't expecting it, and she plowed into him, knocking him to the floor.

Tania turned and ran out the back door. Linda was trying to hold Jett down, and Larry and my mom were trying to pull her off. I turned and dashed out the door after Tania. I wasn't sure where she thought she was going. There was nothing in this direction, so it would take a long time to come to a town or city. She would never make it.

It wasn't hard to overtake her. Tania may dress to impress, but I was in much better shape. I grabbed her shirt and pulled backward. She fell back, and we both landed on the dirt. I grabbed her and tried to hold her down. She kept squirming, and I felt her fingernails more than once. I finally got the upper hand and sat on her stomach and held her wrists above her head.

"How can you do this to family?" she cried.

"Are you serious?" I asked. "You tried to get me thrown into jail for something you did!"

"Most of it was my mom."

"Not all of it. You had someone blow up my car!"

She struggled some more, and I tightened my hold on her wrists. It was all I could do to keep her down.

Tania relaxed and stopped struggling. I wasn't going to let my guard down. "You can't turn in family, Ivy. If you don't press charges, everything will be fine."

"Um...even if I don't press charges, you will still be in trouble. Your mom killed Uncle Rob! The law doesn't care if I press charges against that. She's going to jail. And you tried to help cover for her."

"Not for murder. At least not that I knew of at the time."

"I can't believe this is all for the diner. It's ridiculous." I was getting uncomfortable in this position. "You need to turn yourself in. If you don't, what is going to happen? I don't see you living in hiding."

Jett came jogging over. "I have Linda handcuffed in my truck. You can let her up." I rolled off and sat on the earth.

Tania stared up at the sky with a massive frown on her face. "This isn't fair. Now Ivy will get the diner."

Jett shrugged. "Probably. That's not my choice. You need to come with me, Tania."

She sighed and sat up. "How long will they lock me up? I didn't do anything compared to my mom."

"That's also not my decision. Come on, let's go."

Tania stood and allowed Jett to place handcuffs on her wrists. I watched as he led her around the house. It's good I wasn't completely smitten with Jett. He might start avoiding me and my crazy extended family.

I walked back to the house and met my mom at the door. She placed an arm around my shoulders. "Well, it's been a crazy day. I know I'll have a breakdown later, but for now, I'm starving. Let's eat some of those enchiladas, then figure out what we need to do next."

I nodded and let her lead me into the kitchen. Sitting in Linda's kitchen while she was being hauled off to prison felt funny. I knew this was worse for my mom than for me. She'd lost her brother and now her sister.

We sat at the table, and I smelled the food. It had smelled superb before, but now I wasn't sure I could swallow any. I was relieved it was all over, but that didn't make it all feel happy. I was glad there was no chance of me ending up in jail now.

Chapter 24

The triple chocolate brownies were almost more than even I could take, but I would manage. I grabbed a jar of peanut butter from the pantry and spread some on top of my brownie, then took a big bite.

Jett came in and wrinkled his nose. "Did you really just frost your brownie with peanut butter?"

I couldn't answer because my mouth was full of sticky goodness. He'd picked a horrible time to come in. My mouth was almost sealed together, and it would take a while before I could talk without it all showing in my teeth. After placing the brownie on a napkin, I went to the fridge and pulled out the milk. I poured some into a cup and swished it down.

"You should try it," I told him.

"No thanks. That's really weird."

"You can't say that until you try it."

"Can I take some more brownies out? Those gals out there can really put them away."

I smiled without my teeth and grabbed a tray. I was sure my teeth were still covered. "Here you go." He took it and left the kitchen. Today was Barbra's birthday, and she had rented out the diner to celebrate. Most of my Zumba class was out there with some other people I didn't know.

Muddy Creek was growing on me, but I wasn't sure whether I should stay. Mr. Piper had reevaluated Gramma Sue's will and decided that the diner should go to me since Linda would probably spend the rest of her life in jail. I needed to decide whether I wanted to stay here. If I did, José would help me create a menu from which people could order. Since José was helping, there would definitely be bacon with any choice of breakfast.

My mom stayed with me for a week and then went back home. It had been three weeks now since Linda and Tania were arrested. I refused to take any ownership of Linda's things, even though Mr. Piper said that the house should be mine according to the will. I told them to sell it and transfer it to Tania's accounts. I hoped she would reform herself, and then she'd have something to start with when she got out of prison.

I was going to sell Rob's house as well, and if I stayed, I would remodel my room. Staying at the diner made sense if I was going to work here. I didn't need an enormous house for me and Creepers. Creepers was content to spend most of his time in the window. I still took him out every day, but he just meowed in protest.

"Hey, Ivy," Boyd said, poking his head through the door. "We need you to judge the brownie-eating competition."

"Brownie-eating competition? That sounds messy."

He smiled. "It will be."

I washed my hands and went out into the dining area. Barbra, Opal, and three other women sat at the same table with a plate of brownies in front of them.

"You are all going to be sick," I warned. "I can hold my desserts, and I struggle to eat more than three."

"I think you should join us," Barbra said. "Carol can be the judge."

"Sure thing," a woman in a cat sweater said.

I shook my head. "I'll just watch."

Jett's eyes sparkled. "Wimp."

I tilted my head. "I don't give in to peer pressure, and I don't see you joining."

His smile grew. "I can't."

"Why not?"

Barbra winked. "Because he is the prize."

I laughed. "What is that supposed to mean?"

"The winner gets a kiss from the sheriff."

My heart started pounding, and I was sure I lost all color to my face.

Jett wagged his finger at Barbra. "On the cheek."

"Oh fine," she muttered. "And I'm going to win. It is my birthday, after all. Sit down, Ivy."

"Nope." I wanted to, and I wanted to win, but I could imagine how horrified I would be if I did. I didn't want the sheriff kissing me, even on the cheek, in front of all these people.

"Whoever eats all the brownies on their plate first wins!" Boyd announced. "And no milk. If you need milk, you're out."

Each plate held six brownies, and I was almost sure none of them could finish.

"Ready?" Boyd asked. They all nodded their heads. "GO!" The women all dug into the brownies with a vengeance I didn't expect. Some people from the audience cheered them on. I saw Darcy and Netty Peterson sitting at a booth, far away from the others. Darcy was smiling, but she looked sad. I went over and sat by her.

"You should have joined," she said.

"I don't want a bunch of people staring at me while I stuff my face."

"I know what you mean."

"How are you doing?"

"I'm fine. I've got a job interview in Topica, so I might be moving."

"That's pretty far."

"It might be good to get away from my mom. Hey, can I ask you something?"

"Sure."

She looked down at the table. "You can say no if you don't want to do it. I just thought you did such a good job figuring out the things with Linda and Tania. You must have a talent for it."

"For snooping?"

She shrugged. "My husband disappeared a long time ago. Everyone told me to let it go, that he was probably no good. The police wouldn't do anything because they figured he ran off."

"I'm sorry."

"I know he didn't. He wasn't like that. He wasn't perfect, but he wouldn't just leave. I'm sure something bad happened to him. Will you try to figure it out?"

My eyes widened. "Figure out what happened to your husband?"

"Yes. No one else will."

"I'm not a detective. I don't really have any skills."

"But you solved this last case. Could you at least try? I'll pay you."

My lips moved from side to side as I thought. "Can I think about it?"

"Yes."

A cheer went up from the crowd, and I turned to see Barbra jumping up and down, her pink ponytail bouncing. "I win!" I smiled. She had brownie all around her mouth. She wiped it on her sleeve and punched her arms in the air in victory.

Darcy laughed softly. "I can't believe anyone could eat six of those."

Jett walked up and kissed Barbra on the cheek. Another cheer went up.

"And this side," Barbra instructed, pointing at her other cheek. Jett leaned over to kiss her cheek, and she grabbed his head and kissed him on the mouth. Everyone laughed, and Jett's face turned three shades of purple. The crowd roared in approval. I couldn't believe he hadn't seen that coming.

Jett shook his head and gave Barbra a half-hearted lecture, then disappeared into the kitchen.

"I better follow him," I said.

Darcy smiled. "You should have competed."

"No way. Hey, can you text me information about your husband? I'll see if I think it's something I can work on."

"Sure. Thanks."

I nodded and went back into the kitchen. Jett was leaning against the counter.

"That was fun," I said, trying to keep a straight face.

He ran a hand over his face. "That was so embarrassing. I should have seen it coming. I know what Barbra is like."

"Are you a couple now?" I teased.

He laughed. "She's old enough to be my great-grand-ma."

"You didn't answer the question."

He shook his head. "Have you decided whether you're going to stay?"

"I think I might. I don't have anything to go back to, and I do like the people here."

"You should get qualified and become my deputy."

I chuckled. "That would mean I would have to follow the rules."

"Yeah, that's not really your strong suit."

"Do you have any ideas about what happened to Darcy Peterson's husband?"

"No, I wasn't living here when he went missing. Wait, are you trying to figure that out?"

I shrugged. "Maybe."

"Hmm. Well, good luck. That was years ago."

"If you want to help, you can be my deputy," I said with a sly smile.

He pointed at his badge. "I'm always the sheriff."

"If you say so."

He wiped his mouth. "I can't believe Barbra."

"You know, any of those women would have done the same."

"Probably. They're a funny bunch. They sure keep things interesting around here."

"I wish I'd recorded it."

"I wish you'd entered and won." He winked at me and went back into the dining area.

I wrapped my arms around myself and smiled. I was definitely staying in Muddy Creek.

Ivy's Chocolate Chip Cookies
3 melted sticks of butter
3 cups brown sugar
2 cups powdered sugar
6 eggs
6 tsps vanilla
8 cups flour
3 tsp baking soda
1 1/2 tsp salt
Liberal amounts of chocolate chips
Melt the butter and mix with sugars. Add LARGE eggs and vanilla. It will not work correctly with small eggs. Mix. Add flour, baking soda, and salt. Mix. Add liberal amounts of chocolate chips, or to your liking. Bake at 320 degrees for 14 minutes.

About the Author

Kristy Dixon started writing stories when she was seven and never stopped. She enjoys writing cozy mysteries and YA. At home, she spends her time playing board games with her husband and kids and writing. Occasionally she takes part in a Super Mario marathon. She has six chickens and a cat that help keep life amusing. If she isn't playing with her kids or writing, she is usually eating cookies, or wishing she was eating cookies.

www.ingramcontent.com/pod-product-compliance
Lightning Source LLC
Chambersburg PA
CBHW032303310726
48973CB00008B/2501